4 Short Stories

by

Maury Patrick Roche

ISBN: 1-4033-6214-9 (e-book)
ISBN: 1-4033-6215-7 (Paperback)

Library of Congress Control Number: 2002093747

This book is printed on acid free paper.

Printed in the United States of America
Bloomington, IN

1stBooks - rev. 10/29/02

A trip to America

By Maurice P. Roche

Grandpa tell us again how Great Grandma came to America, Please.

Ok, but remember it, because this will be the last time I will tell you.

Green Ireland, beautiful Ireland. Of course rain makes things green, the grass, the trees and other such vegetation. Ireland gets plenty of rain from the clouds coming from the west over the Atlantic ocean. The first land the clouds come over of course is Ireland. The temperature change in the atmosphere releases tremendous amounts of rain on Ireland. That's why England refers to Ireland as, "Our little umbrella."

Oh well! What I want to tell you about is Your Great Grandmother, Mary O"Donnell. Her parents had twelve children. Seven girls and five boys. Mr. O"Donnell wasn't a big man but he was strong physically and strong mentally.

He was an excellent farmer and worked him self and the rest of the family very hard. The O"Donnell farm was located in County Mayo in the western part of Ireland. The year was 1909. Modern methods of farming were many years away. They worked from sun up to sun down and that required four meals a day. The work was hard, and all were lean and strong.

Two of the boys, Matt and Tom were very good boxers and fought in the ring, usually in the town of West Port, on Saturday nights. There were times when Matt or Tom had no one to spar with in their boxing ring located back of the farm house. Their brothers not being available, they could always depend on Mary. Yes, their 19 year old sister, to put on the gloves. Mary was in the ring sparring with Matt as Mrs. O"Donnell approached. Mary turned to say something to her mother, when Matts fist hit her in the right eye. Down she went.

"What in heavens name are you doing to your sister,?" screamed Mrs. O"Donnell.

"I'm sorry Mary, Oh I'm so sorry, I didn't mean to hit you that hard. Mother I had no intention of knocking Mary down. Mary do you forgive me?"

"Of course I do Matthew, but if I was you I'd be on my guard from now on."Mary replied.

Mary went in the house to help her mother with the usual work done by the women.

Your Great Grandmother ended up with a black eye. She said explaining the black eye to people was one of her most embarrassing times.

Every night after supper the entire family said the Rosary. If a neighbor came by to visit or any other reason and the family was saying the rosary the neighbor would join in. It was a way of life for everyone. I think you should know why the Catholic faith is so important to the Irish people. Many years ago the English tried to do away with the Catholic religion in Ireland. Oliver Cromwell and his English soldiers came to Ireland and destroyed every Catholic church they came to. Cromwell thought, now the Irish will not have their churches to pray in and so they will lose their Catholic Faith. Boy was he wrong. What the people did was make every home a church. They hung paintings on the walls of Jesus, Mary or the Saints. They burned candles, and they prayed, especially the holy Rosary. Cromwells idea backfired on him. The faith of the Irish was stronger than ever. Remember this children. When the Irish left Ireland, they weren't told to make a fortune, but they were all told by their parents, brothers, sisters and friends," KEEP the FAITH"!

One day Mr. O"Donnell said, "Mary go tell your sister Ann to come to the parlor."

"Ann! Ann, Father wants you in the parlor. He has a gentleman with him, you know what that means". Ann went to the kitchen to look in the mirror. Satisfied, she walked into the parlor. Sitting there was a man of about forty years of age. Ann didn't like what she saw.

Her Father got right to the point. "Ann I want you to meet the man who is going to be your husband. His name is Thomas Quinn, Tom this is my daughter Ann."

"I'll not be marrying the likes of him." Ann replied in a very defiant tone. She folded her arms and stood her ground, and waited for her Fathers wrath.

"Tom, I'll be asking you to leave now lad, as I want to have a word with me daughter. Never in all me born days did ever I think that one of my daughters would be so obstinate. I don't know what happening to the children of today. Where, where have I gone wrong?"

Her Father couldn't get her to budge. Ann had a mind of her own. This is just how he taught his children to be. Honest, conscious of God in all things, good work habits and then go ahead and do the right thing without fear. That's just what Ann did.

Later Mary spoke with Ann. "I understand you didn't care for the lad, we could hear Father all the way to the barn, but I knew you wouldn't change your mind. I want you to know that I plan on going to America as soon as I can."

"Mary you can't go until Sara sends the money. It's been almost a year since she left. When she earns enough money she'll send it. Oh Mary, with you gone that will be three sisters in America, how we will miss you."

Mary said, "Ann I plan on going to England and work as a servant, and save enough money to buy passage to America, how does that sound.?"

"I think it's a grand idea, Mary. Your 19 years old and Father will be bring some one home for you as your approaching spinsterhood. I'm 24 years old and a spinster, time is running out for me. Go to America Mary and take the blessings of all the family with you."

At the supper table a few nights later Mr. O"Donnell announced to the family that Mary would be leaving for America with a stop over in England to earn her passage. All the boys agreed to shear extra sheep to pay Mary's way to England. Mary's passage to America would cost about $25.00 in American money. Quite a large sum of money.

Young folks leaving the farm was a normal occurrence in Ireland. The farm was always left to the oldest son who would then take care of his parents for the rest of their lives. The rest of the children would seek their fortunes elsewhere.

Mr. O"Donnell stated flatly that there would no wake held for Mary. Many of the Irish held a wake for the one leaving Ireland, for hardly any one ever returned. Oh those sentimental and tender hearted Irish. No wonder the world loves them so!

Mary's going away party included many,"Keep the Faith," words of advice.

When Mary arrived in London she wasted no time in finding a job. The employment agency placed Mary in the home of Lord and Lady Reginald Cornelius Peabody III as a servant of the lowest class. Mary was surprised to find that the high ranking servants actually used the new help as their own servants. The pay was small, the hours long, but this was what Mary expected. She was given her room and board, that allowed her to save her wages to buy passage to America.

All the young servant girls were very friendly and gave Mary advice by the bucket full. Watch out for this one, that one is a snitch, that one over there is really nice, and so on. The one person that Mary liked the most was the accountant for the estate, Mr. David Goldstein.

He was about 50 years old, bald and with a little pouch on his stomach. His hobby was photography. David told

Mary that he was asked to take many pictures of Lord Peabody. The Master had a very large ego, and considered himself quite a ladies man.

Three weeks after being hired an incident occurred that would change Mary's plans. David had two cameras set up in front of the grand staircase to take pictures of Lord Peabody. Mary walked to the stairs and was only a few steps up when his Lordship stepped up behind her, reached forward and pinched her backside. Mary turned around and as she was still walking down, she through her fist. Hitting Lord Peabody in the side of the face. He was knocked completely off his feet. He lay on the floor stunned.

"You wench! You Irish wench!"he screamed at her as he rubbed the side of his face. "Goldstein, Goldstein, come here you idiot!

"I'm right here your Lordship," Goldstein answered as he gazed down into the furious eyes of his Master.

"You saw what this wench did, did you not?"

"Indeed I did Sir, I'm your witness to this brutal attack Sir." Goldstein replied with a tone of pity in his voice.

Mary looked at David with disbelief, Some friend you turned out to be she thought.

Lord Peabody said,"I have some business to attend to right now. I want both of you to be in my study at two o'clock. Goldstein I want you to have a written statement of Mary's attack. At that time I will decide her punishment." He gave her a glaring look and departed.

David gathered up his photography equipment and was gone in no time.

Lady Peabody in the mean time had observed the complete incident from the balcony above. She felt very sad for Mary, but she was thrilled the way Mary handled the situation. For years Lady Peabody had put up with her husbands philandering but was too fearful to do any thing about it.

At two o'clock Mary and David were in the study waiting for his Lordship, neither one speaking to the other.

A little after two Lord Peabody entered the room. He walked quickly to his desk, sat down and turned to Mary. Pointing his finger at her he stated," You girl will never work in England again and as further punishment I will deduct half the wages you have coming. Now Goldstein read out loud your deposition."

David stood up with the script and said he would skip the preliminaries and get right to the heart of the matter.

"Get on with it man, get on with it,!" Lord Peabody shouted impatiently.

Mary sat up right, hers hands on her lap. Her lips were tight as she looked at David.

David began. "As I prepared to take photographs of his Lordship at the foot of the grand staircase the newly employed servant girl Mary O"Donnell walked past and started to ascend the stairs. His Lordship then followed up behind, reached forward and pinched the bum of the servant girl. His Lordship then walked back to the bottom of the staircase and stood there laughing. The servant girl, Miss O"Donnell turned, hesitated for a moment then came down the steps. In a flash she swung her fist with all her body weight behind it. Her fist hit his Lordship in the side of the face. with such force that a "SPLAT" could be heard echoing off the walls. His feet came completely off the floor and down he went. So stunned was his Lordship, that he was unable get up for a minute or two. This I, David Goldstein, swear to be true. I have in my possession the photographs of the pinching of the bum and the flattening of his Lordship Reginald Cornelius Peabody III. David looked at Mary and winked. Mary's face was all smiles.

"You fool, you idiot, that's not what I wanted," Lord Peabody screamed. "I order you to bring to me all the photos and the negatives and you will rewrite the deposition to my satisfaction, do you understand,? you ignoramus!

"Lord Peabody, with all due respect Sir I would like to inform you of what is going to happen". David stated with firm conviction in his voice. Mary is going to America not Ireland. I have decided to go to America also. It would be a fine demonstration of your character and generosity Sir, to provide us with the funds to purchase the tickets for the voyage."

"Ha Ha! Oh! Goldstein, Have you lost your mind?" Lord Peabody said as he sat back in his chair chuckling. "I have a good mind to have the two of you handed over to the sheriff."

"I don't think so sir, You see those photos could be sold to the London Globe magazine. They would be delighted to buy them. Don't you think?"

His Lordship jumped to his feet. "I'm the president of the Royal Boxing Association, That would make me the laughing stock of all of London. Goldstein this is black mail."

No one had noticed that Lady Peabody had entered the room and sat quietly in the corner during the entire undertaking.

"Give them what they want Reggie, I couldn't stand the humiliation." Lady Peabody knew her insistence would help her husband save face, also she wanted to aid Mary. She would assist this fine Irish girl in her quest no matter what she had to do.

Lord Peabody was delighted to settle this embarrassing predicament.

"Very well, for you dear we'll end this foolishness, I'll pay for steerage for the two of them. Goldstein where are the negatives and photos?"

"There at my brothers house in London, I sent them there with a delivery man." David replied.

"How clever of you." his Lordship sneered.

Goldstein interrupted," We'll need money for train fare to Liverpool and for meals."

Lord Peabody was furious,"WHAT!" he screamed.

Lady Peabody stepped forward, "Very well Mr. Goldstein, The money will be ready when you return with the negatives and photos."Her Husband hurried out of the room shouting, "get them out of my sight."

Mary looked at Lady Peabody with a look of disbelief," I can't believe I'm on the way to America"! She said.

Lady Peabody put her arms around Mary and gave her a very big hug."I wish you a world of happiness Mary."

As the train rolled through the country side to Liverpool, Mary sat staring out the window. David was checking and rechecking the ships sailing schedule.

"We should be able to book passage on the Roratania, which leaves port at noon tomorrow for New York. There's always room for third class passengers. Things are looking up Mary."

"I'm really glad that your coming along to America with me David, although I do believe your a little bit of a scoundrel."Mary murmured. They smiled at each other, and the train rolled on.

It was late when they arrived in Liverpool. After having a meal they made their way to the dockside hoping to be allowed to board that night, but that was not to be. They didn't have their tickets and couldn't purchase them until tomorrow morning.

In the waiting lounge on shore David was able to store his camera equipment along with his and Mary's small suitcases.

"Lets go for a walk David, and if we see an inexpensive hotel we could get a good nights sleep," Mary asked with an expression on her face that indicated that it was an excellent idea.

"Are you out of your mind Mary, we shouldn't even be walking around this neighborhood.

"David I'm so tired I don't care where I sleep. Look! There's a hotel and see how inexpensive the rooms are."

"Mary those rooms are above that tough water front tavern. That place is filled with drunks, cut throats and who knows what else. Mary you are so naive!" David said with all the politeness he could muster.

Mary pointed at the tavern and said,"I'm going to lease a room for the night, I don't believe it nearly as bad as you let on."

"Here Mary, take this pistol, my brother gave it to me to defend myself against Indians when I got to America. I think you'll need it more than me.

Mary pushed the pistol away. "Absolutely not David, I don't like guns, they scare me. Listen David, if your not going to change your mind then I'll see you tomorrow morning at the ticket office lounge,"

"Ok Mary, I'll see you at the lounge in the morning, do be careful," David said as he sneaked the pistol into Mary's handbag.

David watched Mary enter the tavern with a feeling that he should do more to protect her.

Mary walked directly to the bar. The patrons were indeed a bunch low lifes, dirty and some of them even drunk. Every eye was on Mary. What was a young, pretty and petite girl doing in this place they wondered!

"I would like to speak to the proprietor of this establishment," Mary asked.

"Your looking at him Miss, Me, Bruce Wellington at your service. What can I do for yea?

"I want to lease a room for the night," Mary replied with a smile on her face. This was an unusual request and Wellington hesitated.

"Please," Mary entreated," I have traveled all the way from London today and I don't know where else to go at this late hour."

"Ok Miss, here's the key to your room. You see those doors up there on that balcony?"

Mary nodded her head.

Well the second door is your room, number 2." Mary thanked Mr. Wellington and walked by tables with characters seated around them that would frighten even the stout hearted. All watched Mary with suspicion. She smiled at every one she looked at, and continued up the stairs to her room.

David was concerned about Mary, he felt that he should not have let her go in that place. An idea came to him when he saw a Bobby walking his beat. As the Officer approached David beckoned him to follow.

"I have something to show you," David said as he lead the Officer to the door of the tavern.

"What's your problem.? "the annoyed Officer ask. David opened the door and pointed.

In a low voice so only the Officer could hear him David said. "Look at that bunch of sinners in there, smoking and drinking the devils brew. You should go in there and stop this evil, immoral, and degenerate behavior."The Officer was not pleased with David's suggestion and told him he should mind his own business.

David then pointed down the street, and in a very loud voice that could be heard throughout the tavern.

"Go back on your patrol." The Officer shook his head, just another nut he thought, and he slowly walked away.

David had the attention of every one. He walked in as though he was in charge. "Who's the proprietor of this dump.?"

"I'm Bruce Wellington and I happen to be the owner of this establishment, and who are you might I ask.?"

"I'm Inspector Goldstein of Scotland Yard. I'm on the trail of young Irish murderess." David made sure that every one in the tavern could hear every word he spoke as he walked around the room. David brought out a photo of Mary that he had taken a few weeks before." Take a good look at this picture and if you ever see this killer notify the police."Fat chance he thought to himself, these people had such hatred for the police that they wouldn't turn in the killer of their own mother.

David when on. "This girl escaped from a mental institution in Dublin over a year ago. Since then she has killed eleven men. Her method is to go to filthy taverns and flea bag hotels like this dump. She leases a room for the night knowing that some stupid, evil moron like you people

will come to her room to rob and do her bodily harm. Well my friends when they come in, BANG! She shoots their brains out! that is, if they had any to start with.

"Remember it's your civic duty to turn this criminal in if you happen to see her."

With that said David walked out the door and down the street and back to the ship terminal lounge. His heart was pounding. Where in the world did I ever get the nerve to do what I just did, he thought. I'll never go near that place again. I must be crazy.

After saying her rosary Mary was undecided whether she should go to bed or go down and have a cup of tea. A cup of tea seemed like a better idea. She picked up her handbag proceeded down the stairs.

Every eye in the place watched Mary descend the stairway and it was so quite you could hear the horses passing by in the street. Mary sat down at a small table in the corner. Mr. Wellington came over to her table. Before he said anything Mary asked,"May I have a cup of tea please?" Looking down the owner noticed the pistol in the handbag.

"Sure Miss, your tea will be ready in a minute." He went back to the bar wide eyed. "She has a gun in her handbag he whispered to his bartender. The word was passed around and Mary felt uncomfortable with so many of these men looking at her.

"Mr. Wellington would you kindly have my tea sent up to my room please?"

"Very well Miss," Wellington answered. Looking at his bartender he said,"Dick would you like to take the cup of tea to the nice lady?"

"Not on your life," he replied with a sneer on his face.

The tea was ready but there were no volunteers to deliver it, not even for a free drink.

The door opened and in came one of the regular drunks, Derelict Darrell.

"Hey Derelict, how about delivering this cup of tea to the lady in room two?" Wellington ask.

"What do I look like a butler?" Derelict snapped back. Wellington replied, "if you do, the first ale is on the house.

"Why didn't you say so, give me the tea." Derelict was on his way.

Mary was sitting on the edge of the bed examining David's pistol she had discovered in her handbag.

There was a knock on the door, and a voice called out."I have your tea here lady."

"Come in," Mary answered.

Derelict came in and asked,"Where would you like me to set it?"

"Right there on the little table," Mary said as she pointed with the pistol.

BANG! the pistol went off shattering the tea cup.

Derelict made two quick moves. One with his feet, the other with his bowels. At the sound of the shot the patrons looked up to see Derelict come down the stairs like a man

possessed. He ran through the tavern holding the seat of his trousers, his eyes as large as saucers, and out the door he had come in through just a few minutes earlier. Every ones attention was now room number 2. They saw Mary walking out. She walked to the banister, smoking gun still in her hand. Looking at the crowd she said.

"I almost killed him, I"m sorry, I just missed him by inches! Oh if I could do it over again I'd be more careful."

At almost all the tables the patrons were murmuring words like. She's a cold blooded killer if there ever was one. She's sorry she missed him. The nerve of her, she wants another chance. That Police inspector knew what he was talking about. One drunk said to his buddy.

"I say mate if I happen to fall asleep wake me up. I don't want to be here if she decides to come down for another cup of tea."

"Mr. Wellington!" Mary shouted," I believe you should come up here and assess the damage I caused."

"NO, NO," Wellington yelled back. "That won't be necessary, You'll not be charged for damages.

In a low voice the bartender whispered to Wellington,"Why don't you take up another cup of tea to the nice lady?"

"Shut your mouth or you'll be the next one to have a bowel movement", Wellington sneered.

Mary was pleased with his answer. With a big smile on her face she said,

" Good night Mr. Wellington and thank you." She paused for a moment, looking at the motley faces below she said,"Good night gentlemen." only one person spoke, and he uttered,

"I wonder what she meant by that?"

The next day Mary was up early. The only people in the tavern as she paid her bill were the breakfast clubers, having their ale.

Mary hurried to meet David at the terminal lounge. When she walked in she could see that something was wrong.

"David you look tired, didn't you get any sleep?" Mary asked.

"Mary I was mugged last night and they got some of my money but, not much.

"Did they hurt you?" Mary asked with deep concern.

"No, I'm ok Mary, just tired. Let's get something to eat. Then we'll sell one of my cameras for extra money, how does that sound?" he asked.

"Fine," Mary replied, "and don't forget to sell your gun, I have a story to tell you about it later on."

After breakfast they went to the pawn shop and sold the camera and the gun. Next they purchased their tickets for steerage passage to America.

"Look at that poster Mary." David was pointing at the picture of the ship they would be sailing on, the beautiful S.S. Roratania with a photo of Captain Edward Gray in the back ground.

"I have an idea Mary, lets go over to that wireless office across the avenue." David was smiling at Mary as they walked in.

"David your up to something, I hope it's legal, is it?" Mary asked with a doubtful voice.

"Our voyage won't be boring, I can assure you of that," he replied.

David ordered a telegram to be sent to himself on the Roratania three hours after the ship set sail. The telegram read as follows:

DAVID, INCLUDE CAPT. GRAY IN STORY OF

TRIP TO AMERICA

W R H

After they were settled in on board ship, David told Mary from now on she was his secretary.

"I don't know how to be a secretary," Mary answered." I don't have pencil or note pad, nor do I have the desire to be one."

"I'll take care of every thing. From now on I'm a reporter for a very large American newspaper conglomerate.

I'm on special assignment, on how well steerage passengers are treated

compared to others in first and second class. Come on Mary we need an accomplice. Some one who works aboard the ship.

"Should we be up here in first class?" Mary asked.

"Just act like you belong here and they won't question you David answered as he looked at one steward after another."

Mary whispered,"how about that tall fellow?"

"No Mary, see how fussy he is straightening chairs, rearranging the flowers. what we need is some one like that steward leaning against the wall picking his nose. I saw him snitch a cracker from the table. He's our man. It's time to put him to the test.

David walked up to the steward holding a pound note in plain sight.

"I say my good fellow do you suppose it's possible to obtain a maids apron without anyone elses knowledge?" David slowly moved the money back and forth.

"That is no problem at all Sir," the steward said as he eyed the pound note. David had his man.

"I'm David Goldstein and I will have need of your services during the voyage. Would you agree to be so employed be me?"

"Blimy Sir, it would be a pleasure to serve you. Anything you would like me to do, you can consider it done." The steward replied with a devilish look in his eye.

"Very well Pickens your hired." David said.

"Oh no Sir, my name is Higgenbottom, Theodore Higgenbottom.

Looking at the steward straight in the eye David explained."You see the first time I saw you, you reminded me of a Pickens, so from now on I shall refer to you as Pickens."

" Pickens it will be Sir, what ever you say Sir." Pickens responded meekly.

"At three o'clock you will meet me at the wireless office, I'll tell you what I want you to do then," David stated in a firm tone.

When they meet David handed Pickens a telegram and told him to take it directly to Captain Gray himself." Don't give it to any one else, "he was told." Wait for an answer, because their will be an answer from the Captain. Do you understand Pickens?" David asked.

"Indeed I do Sir," Pickens answered, and He was on his way.

After the Captain read the telegram he handed it back to Pickens stating,"This isn't meant for me, it's for a David Goldstein."

"I'm sorry Sir the wireless operator made a mistake, I'll deliver it to the proper person." Pickens responded.

Captain Gray turned to his Executive Officer and asked, "Wilkins, do you know who has the initials W R H and is known almost around the world?"

"Yes Sir, that would be William Randolph Hearst the great and powerful American newspaper tycoon." Wilkins replied.

"Right you are Wilkins, he has a David Goldstein on board doing a story for his organization. We'll give Goldstein our complete cooperation."

Pickens delivered this good news to David.

"You did well Pickens, now tell me who are those gentlemen playing cards they seem to be rather wealth?"

"Those men are very wealth Sir, and they refer to themselves as the BIG FIVE, but we stewards call them the unholy five. They treat the help with disdain and are very demanding, Their wives stay mainly in the ladies lounge. This is the third voyage they have made on our ship. That's about all I can tell you Sir." Pickens answered.

"Thank you Pickens, now I have to find Mary." David left with a smile on his face.

Mary was down in steerage enjoying conversation with ladies from different countries. Everyone was so friendly. Some didn't understand any English at all, but the sharing of cheese, sausage and tea along with smiles seemed to fill the gap. A girl came in and shouted,"is there a Mary O"Donnell here?" Mary walked to her,"Yes I'm Mary."

"There's a gentleman waiting for you outside near the stairs,"the girl replied.

"Mary where have you been? I've searched for you all over the ship. We have things to do. Go get the apron Pickens gave you. Meet me outside the Grand Room on the main deck."

"David what are you up to?" Mary asked.

"I'll tell you all about it outside the Grand Room."

David was pacing back and forth and occasionally looking in the Grand Room watching the unholy five who were playing cards, laughing and sipping wine. Mary walked up to David wearing the maids apron.

"Great Mary! you look Great" David said as he handed her a small feather duster.

"Take this duster and walk around the Grand Room dusting this and that. I want you to take down that picture over there on the far wall and bring it to me."

"David that's stealing and that! I will not do." Mary snapped.

"No, No, Mary I only want to borrow it. I promise you it will be returned. Captain Gray has consented to have me take his picture with his Executive Officer. I have a plan that includes the frame of that picture, now please get on with your part."

"Alright, but I have a feeling there's some thing shady going on." Mary replied with a less than an enthusiastic voice.

""Mary I intend that we are going to enjoy this voyage with the help of the unholy five. Oh by the way, it's also time to give Pickens a few pounds. He's in this for the money you know!"David said with a smile.

"When I told the Captain that W R H wanted a photo of him, I also explained due to the fact that I was staying in third class doing the story of steerage passengers, I had no place to take and develop pictures. Guess what? he assigned a spare cabin for my personal use for the rest of the voyage. We'll have to see about getting a cabin for you Mary." David replied with even a bigger smile.

"I'm content in third class thank you. Mary O"Donnell is not a snob and I'm surprised at the likes of you David Goldstein wanting to be mingling with the high and mighty." Mary's answer

sharp and snappy.

"Oh come on Mary, we're only having some fun on our voyage. Don't be a poor sport. I have to take a photo of

Captain Gray and his first mate now. I'll see you later." David walked hurried away.

"Where would you like us to stand?" Captain Gray asked.

"Captain I'd like you on the left side of this chair and Mr. Wilkins on the right. The first photo will be to check the focus." David replied.

Quickly David walked to the chair and sat down. Captain Gray on one side of him and the first mate on the other. Almost instantly there was a flash. David went back to the camera put his head under the black cover and announced that the focus was perfect. He took two pictures of the Officers and thanked them for their courtesy.

After developing and drying the photos, he took the picture of himself, seated on the chair with a very sobber look on his face, the Officer standing on either side and placed it in the picture frame that Mary removed from the Grand Room. With the picture under his arm he began looking for Mary. When he found her down in third class he showed her the photo with pride.

"Look at this photo Mary, isn't it terrific?" David asked.

Mary stared at the picture in disbelief. How in heavens name did David accomplish this bit of trickery.

"Put on your apron Mary and return it to the place you took it from. Now would be a good time. The unholy five weren't in the Grand Room a few minutes ago." David implored.

"I'll return it David," Mary said," but don't ask me to take anything again."

"Oh! Mary listen, wait to you hear this." David spoke in a very excited voice. "Tonight you and I are going to Dine at the Captains table. I explained to him that this would be necessary in order to do a proper story of the voyage. I informed the Captain that you would be taking notes as you are my secretary."

"David I don't know how to do that." Mary pleaded

"Don't worry, I'll give you a note book and pencil, all you have to do is make little marks

and the Captain won't know the difference. I'll be very interested to know what the unholy five are thinking when they see us dining at the Captains table, especially after they see this picture of me sitting in a chair with the Captain and his Executive standing at my side. Go Mary." David said,"things are happening."

After Mary returned the picture David hid behind some large plants near the Grand Room and waited for the return of the unholy five. When they were seated David walked in smoking a large cigar. After having a drink David walked to the picture. Then turning he yelled, "STEWARD ! STEWARD! COME HERE !!" Pickens who was standing not far away waiting for David's call, responded immediately.

"May I be of service Sir?" Pickens asked.

"Take that picture down at once, and it is not to be hung there again. Do you understand?"David snapped as he walked away in discuss.

Pickens removed the picture and walked by the unholy five who were interested in seeing the photo. They were greatly impressed and inquired of Pickens as to who was this David Goldstein.

"A very, very, important man." Pickens replied as he left the room.

That evening David felt very pleased with himself as he and Mary sat at the Captains Table. Oh yes! the unholy five had spotted him and were busy speculating as to who this David Goldstein was. Mary was taking in the beautiful surroundings as Captain Gray and David made small talk. David would ask about the Captains Life at sea and why he chose this life. The Captain enjoyed this immensely.

David nudged Mary,"Are you getting this Mary?" He said, as he smiled at her with a glance at her note book.

"Oh yes," Mary replied, as she picked up the book and began scratching little marks in it.

It was a lovely dinner. Mary was especially impressed with all the elegant surroundings.

As dessert was being served Captain Gray notice Mary's open note book and inquired.

"What type of short hand is this Mary,? I've never seen anything like it."

Mary was lost for words, but David spoke up.

"Mary's short hand is different because it's Gaelic short hand." David took the book and closed it and handed it to Mary with a look of displeasure in his eye.

"So Mary you know Gaelic, I had a captain once who spoke Gaelic," the Captain said as a gentleman and lady walked up to the table.

"Good evening Captain!" the man said.

"Good evening Doctor and Mrs. McLaughlin," the Captain answered as he stood and introduced them to David and Mary. The Doctor said,"I couldn't help over hear that Miss O"Donnell knows Gaelic. There's not many of us left that know the language. With that he spoke to Mary in Gaelic. David turned white, he was at a lose as to what to do. He just looked at Mary.

Mary looked at the Doctor and with a sober face began speaking in Gaelic. Mary spoke for thirty seconds or more.

"Perfect Gaelic," the Doctor stated," perfect, It's been nice meeting you Miss O"Donnell,

Mr. Goldstein, good evening Captain.

As they walked away the Doctors wife turned to him and said.

"You have a strange look on your face, what's the matter?" The Doctor said.

"I ask the young lady in Gaelic how she was enjoying the voyage and she replied in Gaelic by reciting the Lords prayer."

David was thrilled, Mary surprised him. He would find out later the only Gaelic she knows are her prayers.

David stood up and thanked the Captain for his hospitality.

"Please don't get up," David said, "That story you told us about playing a trick on your captain when you were on your first sea voyage, that was good one indeed. BUT Captain you were a very naughty cadet." As David was saying this he was shaking his finger in front of the Captains face. David knew the unholy five were watching him, seemingly chastising the Captain.

David told the Captain he would have copies of the photos for him and his Executive Officer delivered tomorrow.

David has impressed the unholy five, but there was more to come.

The next day David went to the bridge with the photos and over heard the Captain say to the first mate.

"The sea is calm Mr. Wilkins, so increase our speed to 28 knots and hold it until dusk, then reduce speed to 22 knots."

David had an idea. With this information he searched out Pickens and told him his plan.

Next he went to the Grand Room and waited for the invitation to join the unholy five. It wasn't long in coming. David sipped french wine as he hoped the conversation would get around to the ships speed. One of the unholy five mentioned that he would be pleased if the ship docked on time as he had business to attend to that day.

David said, "Well we'll have to do something about that right now. STEWARD!," he called.

Pickens was there immediately.

"Bring me a paper and pencil please."

As David wrote, he spoke out loud. "Captain, the sea is calm therefore increase speed to 28 knots until dusk then reduce your speed to normal." signed D G

"That should help you some." David said. He handed the paper to Pickens. "Take this directly to the Captain my good man. Pickens was off to a waste paper basket.

"How about a little poker gentlemen?" David suggested with a smile on his face. The game was going along fine. A little wine and idle chatter and a small amount of money loss by David. David was waiting for the Captain to make his usual rounds. He knew the unholy five were dying to talk to the Captain. David spotted the Captain and quickly excused himself as he was running low on money and would have to go back to his state room for more. The unholy five quickly approached the Captain and inquired if the ship was on schedule.

"Oh yes," replied the Captain. "In fact I have just decided that the sea being calm, to increase our speed to 28 knots until dusk then we'll reduce speed to regular cruising speed."

The unholy five walked away stunned. David is one to be handled with kid gloves.

Having observed every thing from behind the potted plants, David was ready to return. When David sat down with the five men he had a sad look on his face.

"Gentlemen an embarrassing situation has just befallen me. My money case was not included when my attire was packed. So I shall have a low profile for the rest of the voyage.

I'm pleased that I'm an not in debt to any of you gentlemen, and I want each of you to know it was a pleasure to be in your company. Now if you will excuse me. I must discuss this situation with my secretary. I certainly don't want the Captain to know of my predicament."

"Oh! Please Mr. Goldstein don't go just yet, "the leader of the unholy five said. "we'll order a drink and my colleagues and I would like confer privately for a minute." Please excuse us

Mr. Goldstein."

David sipped his wine with the thought that all was going as planned. He was very pleased with himself.

The unholy five returned with the Purser and the head Steward. All had a smile on their faces. With a nod from the leader of the Five the Purser stated to David.

"Mr. Goldstein your friends, known to us as the Big Five, have made arrangements for you to charge to their accounts any thing you wish. I have been told to impress upon you the fact that this means you have unlimited spending privileges."

David slowly came to his feet. The look on his face expressed shock, mixed with delight.

"Gentlemen I cannot find words to voice my appreciation of your gracious generosity,"David said softly as he looked at each one of the unholy five.

"Mr. Goldstein you must promise us one thing," the leader of the unholy five uttered with a touch of flair. "You must promise to avail yourself to our offer to the fullest. Do you promise?"

"Yes, Yes indeed," David answered with a smile. "Steward come here." Beckoning Pickens to his side.

"See what these Gentlemen would like to drink and bring me a brandy on ice." The unholy Five were delighted with his first use of their account. That would change in the not too distant future. Pickens face lit up when he saw the generous tip David had added to the bill.

"Gentlemen" David said as he raised his glass to the unholy five, I intend to throw a party in your honor that you will never forget." He touched glasses with each of the sheep that were soon to be sheared as they shouted BRAVO!! BRAVO!! BRAVO!!

"Tomorrow night will be our last night at sea and that is the time I have chosen to have as a gala evening. I will get in touch with the Head Steward to make the arrangements that I will require. I wish this steward to be assigned to me for the party," David said as he pointed at Pickens."

"That will be fine Sir," the Head Steward replied.

David finished his drink and said. "Now Gentlemen I must confide with my secretary, she will be thrilled with what I have planned."

"WHAT! WHAT! a mystery party, David have you gone out of your mind." Mary shouted. "That's insane. Your going to bring the unholy five and other first class passengers down here in steerage for a party and at the same time take steerage passengers up to the Grand Room for their party,? I can't believe what I'm hearing."

"Mary, Mary, calm down, please. I need your help. The people down here in steerage like you, they trust, they'll listen to you. You are the one I need to lead them up to the Grand Room where they will have the party of their lives. Mary why should they be denied this opportunity to see how the other half lives?" David looked at her with sad eyes and a smirk on his face.

"Ok David you win," Mary replied. "Tell me every thing, who's paying for the party? and exactly what am I to do,? is Pickens helping out,? tell me every thing?"

David explained how things would work if every one did their part. Mary smiled at David and said "why not, that will be our last night at sea, let's go out with a bang."

The unholy five and their first class friends were informed that there would be a mystery party tonight and they were thrilled.

As the first class passengers arrived in the Grand Room David made sure that there was no boredom in the atmosphere. The music was loud and lively and all drinks were free. Any drink you wanted was delivered to you free of charge. Pickens did a great job in keeping the drinks flowing. The crowd was in a party mood from the start. David smiled, so far so good.

"Pickens come here", David shouted. "Go down to steerage and tell Mary to bring up as many third class passengers as she can. Tell her to bring them up on the starboard side. I'm going to start the first class passengers down the port side to steerage.

"Come on every body, form a line starting here, your going on a mystery trip," David called out in a loud voice. The line formed quickly, all were ready to get on with the party. Two bagpipers led the way as some ask where they were going, others answered,"who cares," All joined in the spirit of the party. The bagpipes played and crowd followed them down to the bottom of the ship.

Things weren't going so good with Mary. She was having trouble persuading the third class passengers that it was ok to go up on the upper level deck. There was a language problem but that wasn't all, they were just afraid. Pickens saved the day, his waiters uniform gave him an air of authority. Soon Mary and Pickens had a hundred ready to go. Pickens led the way with an Irish man playing the fiddle right behind him.

When David and the first class group arrived in their tuxedos and fancy gowns they were greeted with great pleasure by the steerage folks. The party never let up, the wine flowed, the fiddles played, and the dancing was almost continuous.

The leader of the unholy five was surprised when his wife, filled with wine, did a can can dance. She really did a fantastic dance, very professional indeed, especially when she bent over and flashed her bloomers. It reminded her husband of the first time he met her in a Paris night club.

Now it was the food that the crowd enjoyed. Sausage, Cheese, black Russian rye bread, and numerous other foods. The best wine aboard the ship was sent to steerage, compliments of David Goldstein, that included the food.

Things weren't going so good with Mary and Pickens. Their group sat at the tables not knowing what to do with the pheasant under glass, caviar, and other strange foods. They didn't mind listening to the music but dancing to it, they wouldn't.

David went up to the Grand Room to see how things were going' He wasted no time to change the mood of Steerage crowd. There would be a amateur hour starting right now. He dragged the fiddle player to the stage and saw to it that his intentions were announced in four languages. The people perked up at once, this they understood. David ordered ethnic food and more of the best wines aboard. The party was in full swing and going so well that David had Pickens return to steerage and bring up the first class passengers. David said,"They shouldn't miss this wonderful amateur hour. With the two groups taking turns on the stage the entertainment was fabulous. There was an Irish tenor, an Italian baritone, Russians dancers and much more. Of course the wife of the leader of the unholy five brought down the house went she did her can can dance on stage. Once in show business it's hard to give it up.

Captain Gray watched the excitement with great pleasure, he had never seen anything like this before. He turned to his purser sitting next to him and asked.

"Who's paying for this grand evening? The purser stated that the Big Five had given permission to David Goldstein to charge an unlimited amount to their account.

"These cigars must be very expensive, they are excellent", the Captain commented.

"Yes they are Captain, but please excuse me I have business to with Mr. Goldstein," the Purser said as He spotted David enjoying himself. The cost of this party was soaring higher and higher and it was time to straighten out the account.

David sat across the desk from the Purser and could detect the concern he had regarding the payment due.

"Mr. Goldstein the final cost to you for your party is $8,200.00 American. That includes the orchestra, food, expensive wines and other extras that are listed here." The Purser looked at David to see his reaction.

"Fine, Fine,"David replied with a smile on his face. "I want you to add 15% to the bill. With that money you are to pay yourself $200 00." The Purser sat up and his demeanor changed to one of joy.

"Thank you Sir, and the rest of the money is to go where.?

"Well," David said," Pickens is to be given $400.00."

"Who's Pickens Sir?" a perplexed Purser asked.

"Oh I forgot," David laughed, "His name Theodore Higgenbottom, he is one of your waiters. The first time I saw him he was picking his nose so I gave him the nick name of Pickens."

The Purser forced himself to laugh at what he would consider a crude remark.

"The rest is to be divided among the help that worked on the party." David signed the papers before him and stated, "it's time for me to return to the Grand Room."

"Thank you Sir, Thank You," a pleased Purser murmured.

When David returned to the Grand Room the Captains executive officer was on the stage explaining to the party crowd that Captain Gray received a radiogram from the New York polic department stating that they would be sending a boat out with detectives to come aboard the Roratania to arrest two people for the murder of a dozen men.

" Ladies and Gentlemen please remain calm as the detectives here in front of me place Mary O"Donnell and

David Goldstein under arrest," the Executive Officer shouted. David was stunned and offered no resistance. Mary thinking that this was all play acting snatched the detectives gun from his holster.

"Stand back," she shouted, "So you think we only murdered a dozen do you, well I can tell you it was more like two dozen.

"Mary what are you saying,"? David screamed as the officers held him back.

"Maybe we'll take a few more before the night is through," Mary said as she waved the gun around. Mary was enjoying this play acting to top off this wonderful party on their last night at sea. "You", she said looking at one of the first class passengers, "have you been treating your wife with kindness"? The gentleman starred at the gun in front of his face. He started to turn white. Looking at his wife he pleaded,"Tell her love, tell her how considerate, kind, generous and dependable I am." As he waited for a look of approval on his wives face Mary winked at her and his wife decided to play along with the charade.

"Shoot him he's a terrible husband." she said. With that he passed out and fell off the chair.

Someone shouted,"there's a silencer on the gun." A loud murmur went through out the room.

"Quiet," Mary shouted, with the gun pointed at the ceiling she pulled the trigger. The roar of the shot was startling. Mary dropped the weapon and was immediately taken into custody.

As Mary and David were lead away the Captain ordered the Purser onto the stage to calm down the passengers and even cheer them up.

"Ladies and Gentlemen," the Purser bellowed," Have you enjoyed this expensive and unusual party tonight".?

Everyone responded with a roar of approval, they clapped and stomped their feet. To the Pursers delight he was accomplishing his goal so he continued.

"I would ask a highly respected group of people known as The Un!!, that is I mean The Big Five to come up on the stage." The Big Five stepped forward much to their pleasure. Standing on the stage they smiled and bowed left and right. They still had no idea why they were asked to come on stage, but they loved it. The Purser was about to let them know.

"Ladies and Gentlemen" the Purser began, his arms high above his head and a broad smile on his face."This elaborate and expensive party was possible through the generosity of these fine men, The Big Five. Lets give them a big round of applause."

The crowd clapped and clapped, it seemed as if they would never stop. The Five gathered around the Purser.

"There must be a mistake," they implored, we never sanctioned expenditures for this affair, what was the cost."?

The Purser told them and stated that David Goldstein had their authority to spend that money. They had sad looks on their faces until they saw how their wives were thrilled with the party and showed their pleasure with words of praise for their husbands.

"We have been planning this party for a long time," they explained The Great Party was over.

"What in heavens name is going on," Mary asked, and where, where are we?"

"Your in the New York police department headquarters," the detective explained.

"The officials are telegraphing London's Scotland Yard for further information on the charges made against you by a Mr. Wellington, a tavern owner in Liverpool and one of his patrons, a man called Derelict Darrell."

"Mary it's all my fault," David said as he sat slouched in a chair across the room."I'll tell you about it later."

The next morning David and Mary were told that there was no reason for them to be detained any longer. Scotland Yard telegraphed that charges were dropped by Mr. Wellington an Derelict Darrell when they were told there was no reward and also there were no murders.

As David and Mary were leaving Police Headquarters Pickens arrived. The three of them greeted each other like long loss friends.

"I knew it wasn't true," Pickens said."I just knew it wasn't true". He had a smile on his face a mile wide." The Captain will be pleased to hear this good news, he allowed me to leave the ship and to find out what happened to you. Also I want you both to know that I had sailed across the ocean over a dozen times and have never had should an enjoyable time. Thank you both. By the way, I brought the baggage for the two of you and Mr. Goldstein that includes your photo equipment. the Captain arranged this."

"Thank you Pickens," Mary responded. "And thank the Captain too," David added.

After Pickens left David and Mary were trying to decide their next move. A voice called out. "Mary, Mary." it was Mary's sister Sara and her husband John. David and John shook hands as the two sisters hugged and cried. When everything settled down it was obvious that this would be the parting of the ways for Mary and David. Mary's eyes filled with tears as she put her arms around David'. "Never in all me born days will ever I forget you David. If it wasn't for you I would be still working for passage to America,"

"Where will you be going Mary.?" David asks in a matter of fact tone. Sara spoke up."she'll be going to live with us in the town of Westborough Massachusetts, it's about forty miles west of Boston."

"Well for my self," David said with a big smile on his face,"I intend to go into the photography business right here in the city of New York and I might as well get on with it right now." David hailed a cab and waved good by.

"Do you think he'll be alright,?" John asked. Mary laughed,"David be alright, David will be alright where ever he goes."

As they waited for a cab Mary said," listen to the church bells, it's twelve noon and it's the sounding of the angelus, but no one is paying any attention to it." Mary looked at Sara, John and the people walking by. It was the same way in London."In Ireland," she said, "Farmers would stop plowing and doff their caps as they said the little angelus prayer. Travelers walking the lanes would stop and bow their heads as would the women in their kitchens. This always happened three times a day, six in the morning, at noon, and six in the evening

"Mary, Mary,"Sara shouted. "Things are different here."

"Now I know why when someone left Ireland they always were told to KEEP THE FAITH," Mary answered.

Mary married a handsome lad who lived in the house across the street from Sara and Johns house. It was a wonderful marriage. They had five children, two girls and three boys.

They said the rosary every day. They kept the faith.

And that children is how your Great Grand Mother came to America.

THIS IS THE LOVE STORY OF A UNITED STATES MARINE

By Maurice P. Roche

The names have been changed in this short novel which is based on many actual events that happened in the lives of the following people.

Alexander Joseph Kinnar was born in the small Texas town of Danville in 1911. Alex knew very little of his parents, only what he was told by the kind and motherly ladies of the orphanage, the place he called home. His Mother had died when he was born. His Scottish born Father was killed about a year later in an oil rig accident.

In 1926 on his fifteenth birthday Alex was prepared to run away, he had been planning for this day for two years. He was only able to save seventeen dollars by washing cars and doing other odd jobs. Alex was tall for his age about five foot ten inches and lean. He had a very quite and pleasant disposition to go along with handsome and manly face. It was time to leave,4 oclock in the morning. Last night he said good by to his closest friend. He felt bad about leaving in this manner but had no intention of changing his mind. His distination was the railroad.

He ran through the light rain holding tightly to the little bag which held two sandwiches and an apple. Alex planned on hopping a ride on a train that stopped at the water tower. What luck he thought, a train sat there as though it had been waiting for him. Where was the train going? well what's the difference. The box car was dry and he felt on top of the world, so far it had been a snap..

The train chugged it 's way north all day long. That night when the train stopped Alex hopped off and made his way to a dingy diner for a cup of coffee and a hamburger, then back to the railroad yard, He was in high spirits. The next train was headed west while he caught a fairly good nights sleep. In the morning two very coarse and dirty men climbed into the box car. "Where ya going kid,? they ask. "No place in particular" he answered. "Ya got anything to eat? We ain't eaten nutten

since yesterday," said the shortest of two. "No I haven't," Alex replyed ", but I can give you each a dollar."

Alex reached into his pocket and brought out his small leather pouch, taking out two dollars which he handed to them. The two tramps looked at each with the same thought in mind. They couldn't believe how naive this boy was. The rest of his money would soon be theirs.

They attacked Alex immediately taking his money, then threw him from the train. He landed on a steep slope of small gravel. His body bounced and rolled to the bottom of the ravine, he passed out. When he came to he was looking into the face of a black man. "Don't ya move lad, not until I kin tell if'n you all got ah broken bone or two". Alex was sore and aching, his clothes were torn with a spot of blood here and there from head to toe. The black man looked at him with a genuine gaze of compassion. Alex appreciated this man's kindness and told him so. "Ah seed da men throw ya from da train, and if'n ya was throwed off five seconds later ya migh have landed on dat nice stretch of grass, but that's life." He helped Alex to his feet, "We is going to go to a hoebo camp near by, ya'll be OK after a little rest.'"My name is Alex, what's your,? Alex asked turning his head to get a better look at this kindly man. "Mostly ah is called Utah Joe, but just Joe is find." Joe seemed to be about forty, Alex thought, but he moves about as if he were much younger. "I'm five foot ten so I would guess Joe to be Six foot, I sure like this guy", Alex thought to him self.

When they arrived at the camp there were about eight men sitting around a fire. "Hi Utah" some one shouted. Joe waved a hand, and walked over to the fire. "What's this white boy doing in our camp?" one of the men demanded. "He been hurt, throwed of a train, so Ah bringed him to the camp to rest up some.'''"Well he don't belong here, let him go to the white camp two miles up stream." A couple others agreed. Joe walked to the edge of the woods and picked up a log that weighted over three hundred pounds, and carried it near the fire. He set it lightly to the ground and sat down and rested his head against the log. He made his point, he was very strong and would have his way. The discontents agreed whitey could stay.

Joe Jumped to his feet and shouted," we are going to have a feast." He walked into the stream and retrieved a milk can. It was a large one taken from a near by farm no doubt. "We keep dis milk can hidden an we use it for really good meals." Joe exclaimed. Like a general shouting orders he said, "You two go out and find some fresh corn, shuck and then soak it in the stream." The two were on their feet immediately and on their way. "You two." he said pointing a finger in their face. "Find some potatoes and carrots, nice ones" they were on the way. "We need to come up with seventy five cents to buy some sausage and a chicken, dig deep boys or go find some bottles to turn in for the deposit, that's your job", he said to another two". You know where the Harris farm is, they are good christian people and have always been generous with us, be sure to give them our best." He assigned others to gather fire wood.

Alex and Joe found them selves alone, Joe asked, "Have ya learned anything from you train experience Alex,? "Yah, Don't trust anyone". Alex replied. "Wrong," shouted Joe. "you are going from one extreme to another, what you should have learned is to BE ALERT, that"s right, I said be alert. Know what"s going on around you, Don't go through life with your head in the ground like an ostrich." Alex smiled in agreement. "Joe, my middle name is Joesph and from now on I want to be known as Joe". "so ah'm Utah Joe and you is Texas Joe" he laughed a really hearty laugh, dat's just find with me. Ah guess dis is you way of saying thanks and ah except it. Thank you."

"By the way Joe, I would like to travel the rails with you". Utah Cut him short, "NO WAY"he shouted,"riding the rails is no place for you. You is young and should be getting you self educated. Tomorrow mornin we is going to git you on a train for California, if we is lucky that is.

The fellows were returning with their arms full, Everyone was is a jovial mood, the fire was burning hot. Utah Joe stood in middle of the group and with his arms out streched. "Listen and watch those of you who don't know how to make a hoebo dinner, and Ah will show you. First we be sure the milk can is nice an clean. That can Ah kin assure you, is very clean. Firstly we put in the corn dat has been shucked and soaked in water. We put the corn in standing on edge and we pack in as many as we can git in. Then water is added so as to cover the corn. Next in goes da potatoes the carrots, the cabbage, the sausage and look here we gots a nice chicken dat have been plucked and cleaned just fine." Joe looked around, every one was watching with great interest. "Next," he said, "It's very important to put the lid on tight," A couple of whacks with a small log and the lid was in place. "Look here ya see dis little hole on the top of the lid, ah had dat drilled in there and ah will tell you why. Some one put a penny on the hole, that's it, leave it there. When da fire been burning about fifty minutes the steam inside gonna blow the penny off the hole, dat means leave the cooking continue for another other twenty minutes."

When it was time to remove the can from the fire, Utah, looking around at everyone, says, "don't never remove the lid until da pressure inside has had a chance to release some, dat take only a few minutes. Ah has seen da lid taken off too soon an da food shoot out like a cannon, da sausage was hanging from the tree limbs." All laughed along with Utah.

The meal was not only delicious, but there was enough for seconds for everyone and food left over. The camp area was cleaned up, each person did his own thing, some played cards, read a paper, or slept. Utah suggested that Joe get a good nights sleep, for it was a three hour walk the next morning to the rail yard and he wanted to get an early start.

The next day the sun was rising on a slightly chilly morning. After a cup of coffee the two Joes were on their way. It was near noon when they reached the yard. "That train over there is the one, the one dat is going to take you to California" Utah Joe said. Young Joe knew it was time to say good bye. Utah Joe was well aware of the deep affection the kid had for him. "Ah hates long good byes, so take care of you self," Then with a big smile on his face he added,"Texas Joe." They shook hands and Utah Joe walked away. Joe watched him, he was unable even to say so long.

The train ride to California was pleasant and uneventful. Joe was hungery and his first destination after arrivin in Los

Angeles was to find a restaurant. He walked into Nick's Restaurant an approached the man he assumed to be the owner. "Are you the owner?" "Yeah," said Nick. "I wonder if I could wash some dishes for a meal?." "We don't opertate like that, try some were else," Nick replied. Joe started for the door, a small lady stepped in front of him," Hold on lad, Nick, we need some help in the kitchen, it won't hurt to send him back for a few hours." Joe could tell by the way she handled herself that she was one not to be taken lightly."Go back in the kitchen, don't stand there move."Nick said, "look at the clothes he's wearing, he looks like a bum". Joe looked at Nick. Nick threw his hands in the air, OK, OK but don't feed him until he's through with his work." He walked behind the register muttering," Amy, Amy you would give the place away if I wasn't here".

When they were in the kitchen she says," by now you know my name is Amy my husband is Nick so what's your name?."Joe, Joesph Kinnard," he aswered. "Wash up Joe, and set down at that table in the corner. You look like your starved."He couldn't believe the large steak Amy served him and with all the trimmings. Joe was not unappreciative, he would repay them with a kitchen that would be spotless. Amy and Nick had no way of knowing that the kid in the kitchen was an expert at washing dishes and cleaning almost every thing. He had learned well at the orphanage. As far as Joe was concerned the dish washing wasn't organized very well. He began to work with determination, he would show them what he could do.

Hours later Amy came back, she had been home. "My Oh My," she said, "You've really did an excellent job Joe. Thank you, thank you very much. Nick will be pleased. Don't be surprised if he offers to hire you full time." Joe thought yeah, if he does, I'll bet you had something to do with it. "Finish up what your doing now, clean up. Your done for tonight. Here's a shirt that belongs to Nick it doesn't fit him any more, throw that thing your wearing away."

When Nick came into the kitchen he had a smile on his face. "Nice eh,? Amy ask. "Yea, I been checking up on every now and then. Well kid, would ya like to work steady,? eight hours a day starting tomorrow." "I sure would," Joe replied. "The pay is fifty cents an hour, you start at four to midnight.""And your meal is free," added Amy. Nick shook his head, "Amy, Amy, your no business woman, BUT, he loudly exclaimed," NO MORE STEAKS. We have lots of delicious Ox tail soup and other less expensive dishes, understand.?"Joe nodded his head in agreement. "And another thing, that shirt you'r wearing, it makes you look like a clown, it's got every color of the rainbow on it." Nick was laughing until Amy stated,"That's the shirt you bought in Honolulu two years ago. I gave to Joe, it doesn't fit you any more." "Let's get out of here," Nick Mumbled.

They parted company, Joe walking no where in particular. He was elated, a full stomach, a new shirt, a job, and three dollars in his pocket that Nick had given him. He was sure it was Amy who bugged Nick until he relented and handed over the money. Women are so much more thoughtful and compassionate than men. Utah Joe is a wise man and a good judge of people, he said expect more from women than men, how true.

Joe spent the night sleeping in the lobby of a hotel. After a cup of coffee and a dough nut he went to a St. Vincent DePaul store for a pair of used pants and a pair of shoes. Joe explained to the nice ladies that he only had two dollars to spend. Needless to say the ladies took good care of him.

Things were going good, he was staying at a rooming house and actually was able to save a few dollars. When he has enough money he was planning to move, where? he didn't know yet.

One day on the way to work some one called, "hey young man," Joe looked around. "yes you, come here for a minute." A United States Marine walked up to him with a big smile and his hand held out. He ask Joe if he would step into his office and have a cup of coffee. "Sure, but not for too long, I'm on my way to work." The Marine handed Joe a cup of coffee and sat down across from him". I'm SergeantWilson what's your name.?"" Joe Kinnard," he answered." For the last few days I've observed you walking past my recruitment office. You walk like a Marine, your head is up, and you seen to be very alert. I believe you'd make a good Marine. How's your health.?""My health is excellent,"Joe replied."OK Joe I'll get right to the point, how would you like to be a United States Marine.?"Joe sat back, "Gosh, I never gave it a thought, but I'm pleased that you ask me. Could I come back tomorrow and talk about it.?" "Certainly Joe, and remember if your under eighteen one of your parents will have to sign for you, OK?". Joe nodded with a big smile on his face. Sergeant Wilson knew he practically had a new recruit.

Joe asked Nick how much notice he wanted if he should leave the job. Nick said he could leave any time, but thanked him for asking.

The next day Joe was in front of Sergeant Wilson again, elated at thought of being a United States Marine." How old are you Joe?, you look younger than eighteen." Seventeen," Joe lied. The sergeant went through his usual routine that he had done with many other boys. "Will your parents or guardian sign a waiver to let you join?." "Yes", Joe replied with his fingers crossed.

It was easy to find a vagrant to sign as his father, only fifty cents. Joe was notified that boot camp would start in San Diego in two weeks. He was in seventh heaven. Wow! only fifteen years old and a United States Marine. What would the kids in the orphanage think of him now.?

Nick and Amy were notified. Nick thought it was great, but Amy knew he was too young,

The boot camp training was tough, but the feeling of being a real United States Marine was exhilarating, and boot camp was part of it.

There are some Marines that made Joe feel intimidated. Some were loud and overbearing but most of the Marines reall nice guys. Joe made up his mind to become as strong as he could. He thougth back how Utah Joe picked up that heavy log to send a message to certain people, and they left him alone. "I will be a top notch Marine," Joe had set his goal.

Privat JosephA. Kinnard was learning many things. A Marine never refers to his rifle as a gun, battleships have guns, artillery pieces are guns but Marines have rifles. When Marines chow down in the mess hall it was quit different than in the movies. In the movies the men were loud and without manners. Not so in real life. They were extremely polite to each other, and no one would think of coming to mess dirty. At mess one day a new recruit hollered," DOWN THE RED LEAD"he was really asking for the ketchup. No one moved. He was politely informed of the proper etiquette to be used at a marine mess. That included, never short stopping any thing being passed from one end of the table to the other. For instance, if a person at one end of the table asked,"please pass the salt", that salt goes all the way to the one who requested it without being used by any on else on the way. No short stopping. As in all military outfits the men are addressed by their last name rather than their first, that is until you gain some rank.

Kinnard was able to obtain a heavy duty towing rope which he tied to a tree branch to climb up hand over hand. Some of the fellows laughed as he struggled day after day to improve his physique and strength'en his upper body. Most marines admired his effort and some joined in, to Kinnards delight. He laughed to him self, "here I am only fifteen years old, a United States Marine, and a leader." The encouragement he received from these older Marines helped his self esteem. Things were look up.

In January of 1928 President Coolidge ordered an additional one thousand Marines to nicaragua. The rebels had killed five marines and wounded twenty three. General Augusto Sandino the rebel leader was short in stature but tall conducting guerrilla warfare. It woud be a long war. Kinnard was one of the marines to be sent on this mission, he was thrilled.

The Marine Corp. learned much in Nicaragua. Fighting in the brush, guerilla tactics, living with the bare necessities in the jungle, and so on. The marine flyers were the first to use dive bombing tactics and they did it in Niacaragua.

Utah Joes advice to always be alert was put to constant exercise by Kinnards in his two year hitch in Nicaragua. Many of the marines felt they were troops of the United Fruit Company fighting an unjust war against poor people who only wanted justice. Kinnard put it out of his mind, there was nothing he could do about it anyway.

It was good to be back in California, he was now P.F.C. Kinnar and eighteen years old. He had grown three inches in a little over three years. He was six foot one and weighed one hundred an eighty five pounds. He was also handsome, but he didn't know it.

Gunnery Sergeant Miles, known as Gunny, suggested that Kinnard start working out with the boxing team. "I don't know anything about boxing Gunny," Kinnard explained. "Believe me kid they will teach you". And teach him they did. Kinard caught on fast. The encouragement he received from members of the boxing team made him more determined to be a very good boxer.

Kinnard spent his off duty time boxing, running, climbing his rope, playing cards, reading and drinking beer. He was quite a beer drinker but never smoked. The depression was on across the country, in fact the world.

Kinard not having a family, no wife or children to support, hardly felt any hardship at all. In fact he was able to earn money in different town and cities fighting in the ring. Some boxing matches paid as much as twenty five or thirty dollars. Kinnard was also thrifty, much of earnings were saved.

One day at the Marine gymnasium Kinnard was waiting for a sparring companion, he spotted a red headed marine who did a lot of sparring, but was not on the boxing team.

"Hey red, would you mind working out with me.? "Not at all," he replied. Kinnard sized up his opponent. He was quick in his movements and concentrated deeply. red was probable two inches taller and a few years older than him self, Kinnard surmised.

When they completed their work out Kinnard suggested that they go over to the slop shoot and down a few beers. "No thank you, but I appreciate the offer. I'm one of those Priest that doesn't believe in being one of the boys. I do allow my self the gymnasium work out as a form of relaxation." He held out his hand and said,"I'm Father Daniel O'Neil Catholic chaplin of this outfit."Kinnards mouth fell open, "your a Catholic priest.? Where are your horns,? and your tail.? when I was growing up there were stories of Priest and Nuns. They said if that catholic Al Smith was elected president of the United States he would bring the Pope over here and kill all of us protestants." They laughed and shook hands. "I'm Sergeant Joe Kinnard, thanks for the work out."

Kinnard and Father O'Neil continued to spar now and then, with Kinnard making disparaging remarks about the Pope, Priest, Nuns, and the Catholic church in general. Father O"Neil ignored all of it.

The years went by pretty much the same until things started heating up in Europe. The United States Military began more intensive training. The Marines specialized in amphibious landings so much of their schooling went to this endeavor.

It was 1938, Kinnard was 27 years old. He had no specific plans in life other then being a Marine, this was his home. He was laying on his bunk one day reading a detective novel, which he enjoyed immensely, when Gunny Miles walked in and said,"Kinnard can I talk to you?". "Of course Gunny." Kinnard put down his magazine and walked over to a table where they both sat down. Gunny Miles always had a special interest in Kinnard, hoping to guide him in the right direction. He knew Kinnard was only 15 years old when he came into the Marines 12 years ago. In those 12 years he never received a letter, or a Christmas card, or a box of cookies. He certainly never had a visitor. A number of years he gave up his furlough to a man who had a family to go home to. Gunny thought it was time for him to take a furlough of his own. "Kinnard, why don't you go back to your home town, it'll do you good to have a change,?" Gunny asked. Kinnard answered quickly,"I have never given it a thought about returning to that town, there is nothing there for me, absolutely nothing." "Well at least promise you"ll go some where, OK?"Kinnard paused for a moment, smiled and said,"We'll see." He knew Gunny was concerned about him, and it was appreciated.

Sergeant Joseph A. Kinnard of the United States Marines had his train ticket to Danville Texas, he could hardly believe what he was doing. What would it be like,? who would remember a kid from the orphanage?. Oh well, it was nice just to have a destination to go to.

He arrived in Danville late in the evening and went to the only hotel on main street. It wasn't much, but then it was what he expected. After breakfast the next morning he made sure his uniform was in perfect condition as he was used of doing." This is it," he tought," Danville here I come."

The first land mark that caught his eye was the movie theatre, it looked much the same as it did years ago. It was still in use. The base ball field now had a school on it. As the orphanage came into view he could see it was just an abandoned building. The windows were broken out, weeds were growing up all around the place. The school that was near by was completely gone."well," he thought "so much for coming back home."Kinnard continued to walk around in a leisurely manner. Killing time more than anything. He would go to the restaurant on main street, have a cup of coffee and hamburger and plan his next destination any place would be better than Danville.

Kinnard didn't know it at the time, but entering this restaurant would change his life for ever. He sat down at the last stool that was against the wall. There were two people working, a man about 55 years old and a very fine young lady that looked to be 23 or 24 years old.

"Hello," she said with a pleasant bearing. She looked directly at him and said, "and what would you like.? "Coffee and a hamburger please." he said nervously."How would you like your burger done,?" she asked. "Medium rare," he replied. Kinnard sipped his coffee and watched this lovely lady as much as he could without being obvious. She spent time listening to an older woman who was sitting at the other end of the counter. She very graciously excused her self each time it was necessary to wait on a customer. That girl he thought, she's so refined. A young lad perhaps 12 or 13 years old came in, sat down, dropped his paper bag to the floor and said,"Hi Diane, I"ll have a soda and you can burn a hamburger for me." Diane leaned close to him whispered some thing in his ear. The lad got up immediately and went to the rest room. In a few moments he was out holding his hands high above his head. "There Diane," he shouted, "Are they clean enough now.?" Every one laughed, especially Kinnard, he was very content being here. Kinnard found him self discreetly checking his own hands, yes they were clean. He looked at Dianes face and thought, I'll bet that face is never seen chewing gum, it's just too dignified. As the lunch crowd thinned out Diane was able to have some conversation with Kinnard. After an hour of on and off chit chat He ask her if he could take her to the movies tonight. "Thank you very much Joe, but I couldn't make it tonight. I go to school this evening, However I"d love to go tomorrow night." "That will be great," he said. She could tell he was thrilled by the way his face broke into smile. They made arrangements as to where they would meet, and Kinnard departed.

He went for a long walk, not so much as to take in the scenery, but to contemplate on Diane. The urge to return to the restaurant was immense, but common sense prevailed and he went back to his hotel room. After a nap he read a magazine, then had a shower. It was time to go to the local tavern and have a beer. The bar tender was a very friendly fellow as were the patrons. He was asked why he was in Danville. They were given a short explaination and that satisfied every one, who cared any way. "How about a game of poker fellows,? what do you say Marine.? "fine with me," was his answer.

It was a friendly game, lots of small talk, mostly local stuff. Kinnard was happy, his thoughts were often of Diane. He would not bring her name up in this place. Gunny Miles came to his mind. Thanks Gunny for suggesting this trip.

At midnight the game was still going strong and the owner told them to continue their playing in the back room.

"It's 2 o'clock fellows, lets take a break and have a bite to eat," some one said. Good idea the rest agreed. Chili, hot dogs and more beer was the menu. In a half hour they were back playing cards. Three hours later they all agreed to call it quits for the night or the day as it was going on six in the morning. Outside Kinnard shook hands and said good bye to his new made friends. Each of them going in his own direction. A rough guess told him he had lost about 25 dollars. Still he wasn't depressed in the least, it was a wonderful world.

Suddenly Kinnard couldn't believe his eyes, there across the street was Diane walking very quickly, like she had no time to lose."Where is she coming from, an all night party? certainly not school. Night schools don't stay open all night." He felt sick.

She hurried around the corner and up the steps of St. Lukes Catholic church just as the church bell chimed the six o'clock angelus. During Mass he stayed in the back of the church. He couldn't take his eyes off Diane. Before Mass ended he went out side and waited for her.

"Joe what are you doing here,?" she said with a surprised look on her face. With a feeling of guilt he exlpained that he had been playing cards all night.

She gave him a slight smile and said,"I have to go to work now, you get some sleep and I'll see you this evening."

Kinnard walked to his hotel feeling like a teen ager who has just been forgiven for doing some thing mischievous.

She is a stronger person then I am, why, why?. Not physically of course, but she seems to know what she wants, where she is going, in other words she is in control of herself. Her face reflects that self confidence. That beautiful face.

That evening he met Diane at her house. She explained that her parents and younger sister were in chicago where her grandmother was seriously ill. "Too bad they can't meet you Joe, I know they would like you."

Kinnard was absolutely thrilled just to hold her hand as they walked to the theatre. "What's happening to me he wondered,?. I have never felt like this before in my life. At age 27 he was experiencing LOVE for the first time in his life.

After the movie they went to the ice cream parlor. They sat at a table of by themselves Diane started the conversation by telling Joe about her self. "My last name is Markowsky, and I'm 28 years old. I live at home with my parents and sister. As you know I work at the restaurant in the day time. Four nights a week I go to school studying to be a nurse. There's not much more to tell. If you can think of any thing to ask me please do." she said.

Kinnard told her about running away from the orphanage, joining the marines, his experiences in Nicaragua, and his boxing career. He made reference to the fact that he switched his middle name to his first name."Oh yes," he added,"I'm 27 years old.

She looked at him with a sad pout on her face and said,"I hope you like older women Joe."

He couldn't answer, his eyes said it all, they began to water. She knew his feelings now. There was no doubt he was deeply in love.

"Joe will you get me a coke please,?" she said in order to allow him to wipe him eyes way from her.

They stood in front of her house saying good bye, it was a long good bye.

"What time does your train leave tomorrow morning,?'

"six", he answered.

"Will I see you again,?" she asked already knowing the answer.

"I'll be back as soon as I can, will that be ok with you,?"

"Oh that will be fine, she said as she stepped closer to him.

"It's alright to kiss me good bye Joe, that is, if you want to." He put his arms around her and they kissed. By normal standards it wasn't much of a kiss, but to Kinnard it was an emotional high. True happiness for the first time in his life. Things could not be better.

Back in camp one thing was noticeable to his fellow marines, his very pleasant disposition. Gunny Miles was particularly interested in his trip to Danville as he was the one to suggest it in the first place. Kinnard told Gunny about the girl he meet and that he would go back to see her every chance he got.

Kinnard purchased a 1934 Plymouth convertible with the money he had saved. When he had the time off he could go when he was ready and not have to rely on a train schedule.

It took him 18 hours to drive from San Diego to Danville. It was a tiresome drive, but Kinnard would do it every chance could. On his fourth trip he offered Diane an engagement ring. She readily accepted.

When he drove up to the camp gate the Marine on duty checked his leave papers said,"OK,"and waved him on.

"Would you like to see a picture of my girl friend,?" he asked the guard.

"No I wouldn't, now move on," Kinnar drove off smiling.

On Monday morning Kinnard knocked on the door of the Chaplains office. Father O"Neil opened the door. He was surprised to see Sergeant Kinnard." Come in Joe," Father like to refer to the men by their first name when dealing with them one on one.."Do you have a new joke about the Pope you want to tell me?." "No Father, I want to become a catholic." Kinnard replied.

Father pointed to a chair,"sit down Joe. I"m having a cup of coffee, would you like one.?""Yes I would, thank you." Father O"Neil handed him his coffee and sat down across from him. He looked Kinnard in the eyes and said. "Is she a blonde or brunet Joe.?" Kinnard sat back with a puzzled look on his face and said. "What do you mean.?" Father repeated himself. "Is she a blonde or brunet?

Kinnard paused, looked down at his coffee and said,"brunet." "Joe I love being a priest, I work hard at it. I couldn't convert you to the church if I tried for a life time. BUT a woman, yes a woman has the power to do things a man can not do. Great world leaders who are feared by men are told by a woman to sit down and shut up, or wipe that food off your mouth, or don't wear that, you look silly in it. Women are the leaders of a home, they feed, teach, protect the children. When things are going badly a man might abandon his family, but not a woman. A mother would give up her life to protect the life of her child without giving it a second thought. Us men, well, we'd have to think it over. When Jesus was nailed to the cross the women were there, but the only man there was John. Where were the other men.? They were afraid Joe, they were hiding. Never, Never, Never underestimate the power of a woman."

About becoming a Catholic Joe, you have to take instructions in the faith. After you know what the church believes and teaches and you can accept it, you can enter the church. No one should become a Catholic just to please another person.

Kinnard stood up and put out his hand, "I want to become a Catholic," he said. "OK Joe be here tonight at eight thirty. Two others will be here for instructions with you."

On his next trip to Danville he brought along a beautiful diamond ring, an engagement ring. He wondered if he was rushing things too fast, but he couldn't help him self. He wanted her to be his

wife so much, that he would do any thing to accomplish that goal.

When he presented the ring to Diane he could see she very pleased, in fact thrilled.

"Of course I'll except it Joe, Thank You so much." She threw her arms around him and held on tight. It was Joe who was speechless.

He was going to keep his secret for another time but he blurted out,"Diane, I"m taking instructions to become a Catholic.""Really Joe,?" She paused for a moment, then smiling she said,

"Lets go over to the ice cream parlor and celebrate our engagement and your new religion," She held her ring finger high in the air and just beamed at it..

Joe had never known her to be so happy. He knew now that he was the luckiest man in the world.

Back at camp the training intensified as the troubles in Europe increased. There may be a war so it was Kinnards intention to get married as soon as possible.

It was three weeks before he could get back to Diane. He drove up to her home about four in the afternoon. He noticed that she walked slowly to his car and she looked very serious. He hurried to her and took her in his arms. The kiss was long. She gently pushed him back and a conversation ensued. She spoke for a long time. When she was finished he shook his head no. She spoke some more, her eyes soft and pleading. Again his head shook no. Then he talked for two or three minutes and she shook her head no.

Diane handed him the engagement ring, he refused to take it, so she put it in his shirt pocket. Kinnard said something else, She answered and he turned got in his car and drove off. Kinnard was tired, confused and very up set. It was late, so when he saw a Motor Hotel he pulled in to eat and get some rest.

The next morning he was on the road again. He was a man that had just lost every thing. From now on a smile on his face would be a rare sight. As he was driving along he reached into his shirt pocket, took out the engagement ring and threw it from the car without taking his eyes off the road.

It was nearing midnight when he was approaching the" Horse Shoe Roadhouse". Kinnard pull into the parking lot. He could hear the music, laughter and hollering from his car.

The place was packed on this hot Saturday night, but he managed to get a seat at the bar.

"Whatcha have?", the bartender ask. "beer" Kinnard said as he reached for his wallet.

A bottle of beer was set before him and no glass was offered. All the locals drank right from the bottle and he would do the same. He had a feeling the glasses would be dirty any way.

Kinnard was in a depressed mood as he sipped his beer, when one of the local girls approached him. "Hi Soldier, I'm LoLa Mae, care to by me a drink.?"

"No", came the fast and curt reply.

"My, we're getting a little nasty now aren't we.?" she answered. Kinnard turned and looked at her. She wasn't bad looking, but she had no class at all. The cheap print dress she was wearing was no doubt worn for all occasions, dances, funerals, weddings, corn husking and what have you.

"Just leave me alone," he said and turned back to the bar.

"TINY", she shouted, as loud as she could. "TINY COME HERE."

Kinnard looked across the room and saw a very large man making his way to LoLa Mae. He was about six foot six and at least 350 pounds. The straps of his dirty overalls pulled tightly on his shoulders holding his bellies hugh girth. Tiny's small beady eyes were intense, he didn't take them of his destination. On the back of his head he wore a small straw hat. He had a full dark beard with lots of beer foam on it.

"What's going on here,?" Tiny ask.

"This soldier called me a slut," LoLa Mae lied.

"That, I did not do," replied Kinnard. Tiny paid no attention to what he said. Leaning close enough that Kinnard could smell his bad breath he said.

"We don't cotton to strangers coming in here and calling our sluts, sluts, you understand that soldier boy?"LoLa Mae nodded her head in agreement.

"Your going to give'm a beating aren't you Tiny.?" she asked. Tiny didn't answer he just held up his hand indicating that she should be patient. Tiny was happy to be the center of attention. His only claim to fame was to beat the tar out of some one, and reap the praise and attention of his fellow red necks, especially the girls.

The crowd was starting to get more rowdy. There were shouts of," knock his brains out Tiny."

Some one threw a glass, it hit Kinnard a glancing blow off his forehead. He wiped the blood with his handkerchief. He couldn't make a run for the door, there were too many hot heads in his way. If he only had to deal with Tiny that would be no problem. The crowd was getting louder.

Tiny in center stage raised his arms, an indication. that he was about to take action. The crowd quieted down some. The smile left Tiny's face. With his beady eyes he looked directly at Kinnard.

"Soldier boy, I'm going to let you get any hold you want on me, and then I'm going to squash you like a bug.."

Tiny turned to the crowd for approval and they gave him an encouraging reponse.

Kinnard stood in front of Tiny. Tiny slowly turner his body with his hands high in the air. The smile on his face was a mile wide. Tiny was definitely savoring the monment.

Suddenly the smile left his face, his eyes bulged out, and his mouth fell open.

"What are you doing,? What are you doing,? that ain't fair," Tiny complained.

Kinnard was behind the big guy, he had reached up and took hold of Tinys testicles and held them firmly in his powerful hands. A slight squeeze got Tinys full attention.

"Listen fatso, the first thing you do is to tell those gorillas to move back, if any one of them comes near me I'll tear these things off on put them in your back pocket, understand.?"

"Yes Sir, ah understands, you gorillas move back like the Soldier boy say."

Kinnard said, "And another thing I want you to understand. I am not a Soldier boy, I am a United States Marine, **GOT IT?"**

"Yes Sir you is a New Nited States Marine **Sir**." Tiny replied nervously. Kinnard looked at LoLa Mae,"you girl, pick up my cap and put it on my head backwards." She quickly complied.

Kinnard said to Tiny, "Now listen to what I have to say. You and I are going out that screen door over there. We're going to go through it like a train, understand.?"

"Yes sir like a train," Tiny repied.

"Ok,"lets get going," Kinnard said,"Start saying choo choo until we're through the door." They started slowly, Tiny saying choo choo in a low voice. Kinnard adjusted the volume and Tiny let out a loud **CHOO, CHOO, CHOO, CHOO,** all the way to the door. In the mean time Kinnard was sounding the whistle with a loud **WOOO, WOOO, WOOO**.

They went through the screen door like it wasn't there. Pieces of wood flew in all directions. To neutralize Tiny, Kinnard gave him the squeeze of his life.

Tinys eye balls rolled back in his head and his body fell limply to the ground, he laid there like a beached whale.

Kinnard took off running, for his car, one hand holding his cap on, the other reaching for his keys. He jumped into his convertible without opening the door.

The crowd spilled out on the parking lot and they were furious. Some went to aid Tiny and others threw beer bottles at Kinnard as he drove away. Three or four bottles hit the car but there was no serious damage. No one follwed him. He had about an hours drive to San Diego.

Tiny was helped back into the tavern. Two chairs were put together for him to sit on. He rested his arms on the table with his head bent over so far that his face all most touched the table.

One of the girls said,"Tiny, that fella was littler than you, how come you let him push you out the door like that.?"

"Hush your mouth Sara Lee, you don't know nothing." said LoLa Mae.

Tiny didn't move except for his right fist to come down with a bang on the table. "If I ever see the soldier boy again I'll break him in two."

A drunk spoke up,"You forgets Tiny, he weren't no soldier boy, he told you he was one of them tha Governmen Marines."

Tinys right fist hit the table again. There were those that didn't want Tiny a go on a rampage. "Let's have some music," some one shouted.

"Here's a quarter LoLa Mae, play the jute box."In a short time the place was back to normal, dancing, drinking, laughter and loud talk.

Suddenly things began to quite down until the only sound was the jute box. It was the song that got their attention. The first song that LoLa Mae picked was Chattanooga Choo Choo. Four or five red necks ran to the jute box to press the cancel button.

Tinys right fist come down with a powerful blow on the table. He shook his head slowly. This was just not his day. He didn't know it now, but he would meet that New Nited States Marine Again.

When Kinnard reached San Diego he stopped at a gas station to clean up. A Marine always is presentable, that's the way it's taught in the corp.

Sergeant Kinnard was a different person and it was obvious to all who knew him. No more friendly chats, like how's your family?, when are you going to marry your girl friend.? He could care less.

Kinnard saw Father O"Neil on the company street. "Father I won't be taking any more instructions." He walked away before Father could say a word.

They broke their engagement, Father thought to him self.

Time went on. Kinnards Regiment was sent overseas. When they returned back to California America had entered the war. Japan had attacked Pearl Harbor.

Two new men assigned to Kinnards squad were PFC Pau Charbonneau and Private Patrick Rourke. Charbonneau was 22 years old and had just been married. He already had 3 years in the Marines. He had a very nice personality and a perpetual smile which revealed a slight space between his two front teeth. Charbonneaus main concern in life was his wife.

Rourke was 18 years old, just out of high school, and a little bit cocky. When the war broke out he enlisted in the branch of service that he admired, the United States Marines.

Kinnard was 31 years old now. His physical condition was excellent, and so would his men be under him. Most of the company was made up of 18 and 19 year olds. There were a few 17 year olds, a number men in their 20's. Gunny Miles was the oldest. He could have stayed in the states but insisted on going with his outfit. He was probably 50 years old.

Sergeant Kinnard said to his men,"Some of you think your ready for combat, well I'm telling you your not. We are going to train, and train until you are ready. Tomorrow morning we start at 5 hundred hours. When you get back to camp and you still want go on liberty, consider yourself ready for combat.

When they returned to camp the next day all were exhausted. This country of New Zealand is rugged with it's many hills and mountains. Coming down the steep slopes was harder than going up. You were constantly holding your self back.

All took a shower, but about half the men didn't go to mess, they were too tired. No one went on liberty. That is except Sergeant Kinnard, and he made sure that every one knew he was going.

Kinnard had made his point. He had gained the respect of the company.

It was a week before most started taking liberty.

When their outfit was sent to Guadalcanal, Kinnard showed that he was a leader. A Jap sniper in the ravine to the left and making a nuisance with his periodic shooting. There was no front line. The ravine on the left belonged to the Japs, even though it swung around behind us. The ravine on the right was ours, and it protruded into the Japanese side.

Kinnard checked his twenty shot" Rising Gun", it had a folding handle made of wire. The weapon was made for paratroopers.

Roarke and Charbonneau stepped over to Kinnard and said we want to go with the Sarge. They each had a rifle that was used in the first world war. A springfield 03.

"OK" Kinnard said,"This is the way it goes, I'll take the lead and watch what's in front. You Roark follow me and look up in the trees and on both sides of us. Your going to have to keep your head on a swivel. Charbonneau you bring up the rear, make sure no one gets us from behind."

That was their first patrol into the jungle but not their last. A Jap machine was holding things up. Kinnard said he would take care of it, Roarke and Charbonneau automaticlly took their proper places behind Kinnard. When they reached the right spot Kinnard said,"Roarke make your way up to that large tree and stay there. Fire at them once in awhile to keep their attention. Charbonneau you go to the top of the ravine from the right, I'll go from the left. In about 5 minutes it was over.

When they returned some one said here comes the three musketeers. Not very original, but it was appropriate. All three of them liked the title.

Another time the three musketeers were sent behind the Japanese lines to retrieve some supplies that were left there. Roarke noticed that Sergeant Kinnard was getting more wreckless all the time. Taking chances, and showing a nasty streak. On one occasion Kinnard pumped a couple extra bullets into a Jap after he was dead.

"Was that necessary Sarge,?" Roarke asked. Kinnard said nothing, he just walked away.

The battle for Guadalcanal was over. The Marines were happy to be aboard the ships. No more flies, no more mosquitoes, no more leeches, no more perpetual dampness, no more C rations, no more sleeping on the ground and no more Japanese.

The loud speaker announced that there would be Catholic Mass tomorrow at 0700 hour on the starboard promenade deck. Roarke went to the mass. Father O"Neil was the priest and Roarke was the only one in attendance. Things were really different the night before they landed on Guadalcanal. There wasn't Chaplain on board the troop ship. So they announced that the Rosary would be said at the aft section of the ship. A good catholic with a Massachusetts accent lead the prayers. It was amazing how many Marines showed up. Roarke was pleased to see how many Protestants were there cashing in on Our Blessed Mothers Holy Rosary. It was as though we were a ship full of Monks. Things were different now. The battle was over, the sun was shining. We're heading for New Zealand and all is well. No need to pray now. Father O"Neil would say his masses alone for the rest of the voyage, and Roarke would always remember how hypocritical it was of him not to go to Masses aboard ship.

The men were setting around on the deck talking of many things. Sergeant Seppioni said,"Hey Kinnard, remember when you got run out of that road house and decided to go back and clean the place out.?" Kinnard nodded his head. Seppioni Said." Kinnard asked 10 or 11 of us to go with him to this road house and teach these red necks a lesson on how to treat a Marine. We went in two cars on a hot saturday night, most of us were from the boxing team. Kinnard told us," the biggest guy in the place is called Tiny, he's mine if he's there. You Seppioni and York neutralize the bar tenders they probably have guns. And Kowalski ask," who do we punch out Sarge,?" Kinnard looks at him and smiled,"don't hit any one who looks intelligent."he said." We all laughed."

They went storming into the place, Seppioni and York did their job. Kinnard had no problem finding Tiny and went right to work. Four tremendous blows to the stomach and a few to the jaw and the big fellow was down. He didn't try to get up so Kinnard let it go at that. He looked at Tiny and asked,"do you remember me.?"

"Yes," he replied. Kinnard was satisfied and he turned to see how the rest were doing.. Only five were fighting. The rest remained in their chairs. One incident occurred that saddened all of them. When one of the Marines was taking a swing at a red neck, the guy stepped aside and the Marines fist hit LoLa Mae in the face. She was out cold. Even Kinnard felt bad.

Kinnard said, "Let's get out of here, and that's the end of the road house story," replied Sgt. Seppioni.

The Division reached New Zealand in poor shape mainly because off malaria. When they were back in training things went back to normal. Kinnard was still the loner, Charbonneau sat around and wrote letter after letter to his wife. He went on liberty only once. He went into town, had a dish of ice cream and returned to camp. Roarke went on liberty almost every night, whether he had a pass or not. Life was good, life was exciting.

Roarke would notice Kinnard looking at a small photo of that girl Diane. This would happen periodically, but no one said a word to him.

There were practice amphibious landings at Hawke Bay and other intensive training. The Division would soon be on it's way to their next battle.

That next battle was on the small island called Tarawa. The fighting was ferocious. On an atoll about the size of central park in New York lay about six thousand dead. One thousand of them were United States Marines, another two thousand were wounded.

On the last day of combat, Kinnards company made a charge to wipe out the last of the Japs. As the Marines moved forward through thick foliage a shell landed right at Roarkes feet. It was so close that when it exploded he was in the middle of the explosion and picked off the ground. He went to a near by tree and checked him self for wounds. He didn't have a scratch. Then another shell went off just on the other side of the tree. The tree saved him. He ran as fast as he could through the under brush to catch up with his platoon. He didn't know it but, he had passed the other Marines. Where are the Marines and Japs he wondered. He came to a small clearing and increased his speed. Almost instantly he jumped over the heads of two Japanese soldiers who were in a fox hole behind bushes and a log. Roarke continued to run, fearing a shot in the back.

"What a lousy spot to be in!" he tought, "Behind the Jap lines alone." In less than a minute Roarke was in a fire fight. Years later Roarke would say.

"This one Jap, who was about my age, jumped up on my right and not only shot me, but shot my carbine out of my hands, it was gone. That Jap, he was decent looking guy."

Roarke was shot again before reaching the Marine lines. He lay wounded for about an hour. Then he was shot once more. After three attempts Marines were able bring Roarke in.

Sergeant Kinnard and Corporal Charbonneau were not so lucky. At times, when an assault on an enemy position is about to take place, some Marine will jump up and yell to his buddies, "Well, what do you want to do, live forever,? FOLLOW ME."

Roarke was told that Kinnard stood up and walked right into the bush in front of every one, spraying bullets left and right. At the same time Kinnard was saying something to the Japs but no one knows what it was. He was shot between the eyes. He was dead in an instant.

Charbonneau was hit by a grenade that exploded as it hit his face. Half his head was blown off. This prolific writer of love letters had sent Mrs. Charbonneau her last.

Roarke was sent to the Naval Hospital in San Diego California where he would spend almost a year and a half recovering.

The care the Marines and Naval personnel received at the hospital was excellent. The work that the nures and nures aids performed was achieved with dedication and compassion. Words can not express the warm feeling the Marines and sailors had for these wonderful girls.

It was sunday, visitors day. The few patients that were expecting visitors sat up in their beds, hair combed and all smiles.

One patient, who was ambulatory wanted to have some fun. So he tied a string to his slipper

and pulled it along as though it was his puppy. He asked a visitor,"do you like my puppy.?" Thinkin he was a mental case she said."Why yes, he's a lovely puppy.""If you really liked my puppy you would pet him,." he said looking at her with a sad face.

She bent down and stroked his slipper." Nice boy, nice boy." Just then a marine arrived in his wheel chair." Mom get up, get up. This is Martin, he's just having fun at your expense."

Martin looked at his buddy and said," Sorry Koster I didn't know it was your Mom. I'm sorry Mrs. Koster," he said as he helped her up. Roarke and other patients near by had a good laugh. These kind of behaviors were a tonic to the patients. Roarke heard Mrs. Koster ask Martin, How would you like to have that other arm in a cast too.?"

The magazine article Roarke was reading was interesting enough that he didn't notice some one walk up to his bed.

"Patrick Roarke,?" a pleasing feminine voice inquired. He looked up to see a most elegant lady standing near the front of his bed. Her brunet hair was fixed in an up sweep with a jaunty little hat on top. The green suit she wore had braid around around the collar and edging of the suit. She wore white cotton gloves with cut work at the top. Her left hand held a small white purse close to her side. Her skirt just covered her knees. The green shoes matched her dress. She stood erect with a pleasant smile on her face."My name is Diane and I would like to talk to you."

"Your Sergeant Kinnards girl friend the one that dumped him, aren't you.? Roarke asked." Do you mind if I talk to you about Joe.?"She asked, Not at all," Roarke replied. "I saw him occasionally look at a small snap shot of you, but he never ever mentioned you to any one. We often wondered why you dumped him. It broke his heart you know.?"Roarke looked at her to see her reaction.

"May I set down,?" she ask, glancing at the chair near him. "Oh sure," he said, moving his leg with the cast so he could be a little closer to where she would be sitting. He didn't want to miss a word.

When Diane sat down Roarke did his best to observe every thing about her. First he noticed that she didn't cross her legs, that would be unlady like. He was close enough to smell her perfume and he even recognized that it was, Evening in Paris. His sisters wore it. The perfume wasn't over powering, just a pleasant aroma. Besides it was inexpensive, you could purchase it in any drug store.

It was easy to see why Sergeant Kinnard fell so in love with this girl. She had those three things that men cannot resist. She was NEAT, She was DIGNIFIED, and She was FEMININE. The womem that have all three of these attributes are the ones that men rush to open doors for, to give up their seats on a street car, who hope she will just look at him and smile. Roarke remembered the time he over heard two young women discussing a couple that had just walked pass them.

"Why," one of them asked the other," would a handsome guy like that pick a girl as homely as her.?"

These young ladies didn't understand the three important words. Neat-Dignified-and Feminine. The girl they though to be homely understood and she had it. The handsome guy looked at his girl friend as beautiful. All women who have N-D-F are desirable to men.

Diane looked at Roarke in a serious manner and said,"Patrick, you asked me why I broke my engagement with Sergeant Kinnard. Let me tell you what happened."

The last time Joe came to visit me he had already given me an engagement ring and we were planning on setting a date to get married.

I was sitting on the front porch as Joe drove up. I walked down the steps to meet him. Joe rushed up to me and put his arms around me and he gave me a very long kiss. I tried to push him away in a gentle manner. He said,"What's the matter,?"

I said,"Joe, you cann't kiss me like that any more."He stood back and said,"What are you talking about.?"

With tears in my eyes I said, "Joe I'm your sister." He started to laugh, but he could see I was serious. "What's going on.?" he yelled in a loud voice.

"Joe you and I are brother and sister, come sit on the steps with me and I'll tell you what this is all about."She held his hand and continued." When my parents came home from Chicago I told them about our engagement and they were thrilled. Mom and Dad wanted to hear everything there a was to know about you. When I told them your last name and that you were from the orphanage I thought my Mother was going to have a heart attack. She laid back in her chair and my Father rubbed his hands while he talked to me with a pale face.

"Diane that boy is your brother." Dad explained. He went on about how they adopted me from the same orphanage knowing that I had a brother there. They could only afford to adopt one child. Mom and Dad thought it best not to tell me that I was adopted."

"Joe stood up and walked a few feet, I followed him. He turned around and said."

"My enlistment is going to be up soon, we'll go to Canada and change our names, we'll get married and then be off for Australia."

"Joe we can't marry, we're brother and sister, what's the matter with you.?"

"I don't have a sister" he said.

"The engagement ring he gave me was in my hand, I held it in front of him and said," take the ring Joe". He refused to take it so I put it in his shirt pocket.

Without saying a word he walked to his car and drove away. I never saw him again.

A Psychiatrist told me Joe could not accept me as his sister. If he did he would have to cancel out all the happiness and love he enjoyed in our relationship. This he could not do because it was the only true love and true happiness he had ever known.. I wrote to Joe many times, but never received an answer. I found out about Joe's death because he made me his beneficiary on his insurance. They gave me his private belongings. If there's anything you want Patrick you can have it." "I would like to have that small snap shot of you that he carried with him." Roarke answered.

She opened her purse," I have it right here," and she handed it to him.

"Diane please forgive me for thinking so badly of you. I was assuming that you were the one who was the cause of all his grief and sorrow. Now I know your a very lovely person."Roarke was sad as he said those words.

Diane stood up leaned forward and kissed Roarke on the forehead."I wish you a good recovery Patrick," she said with a smile as she squeezed his good hand. Diane walked to the door and turned around, she gave a little wave of her hand. Roarke waved back. "Just as I thought," Roarke said to him self." The seams of her stockings are perfectly straight".

Roarke was discharged. He went home and married a beautiful blonde of Scandinavian ancestry. They had a large family. Roarke retired as a chief from the fire department of a large easter city. He and his wife are living in a small town in Vermont.

The small snap shot of Diane is in a trunk in Roarkes attic, along with other world war two memorabilia.

Should you ever get to Tarawa go to the Marine Corp. cemetery. When you stand in front of the grave of Sergeant Joseph A. Kinnard, twenty feet to the right and four crosses in, is the grave of Corporal Paul Charbonneau.

Say a prayer for them.........All of them

Reunion

With Revenge

By Maury Patrick Roche

"Tell me about your high school reunion Bob. Are you glad you went?

"I certainly am. Sit down, this will take some time."

Remember me telling you about Helen the girl in my class that went to the prom with her boyfriend, George Van Pelt?"

"freshen my memory."

"Well it was many years ago that we graduated from high school. Helen and George were going steady. He was the hot shot of school: rich, handsome, with a cocky attitude. He had the newest and fastest car. At the prom there was alot of drinking going on and George had more than his share. Helen wanted to go home, but George just kept on drinking. So this gal Bonnie has her own date drive Helen home. Bonnie really took over. She always had a crush on George, but he never gave her a tumble. When he wanted another drink Bonnie made sure he got it promptly. When the party was breaking up Bonnie said George had too much to drink and so she would drive him home. The two of them left with Bonnie driving his car and George passed out next to her. Neither one went home that night. Bonnie drove straight to Bowling Green, Ohio about 200 miles away. They were married about six in the morning. You see Bowling Green is a place that couples can be married without red tape. It's the Reno of the midwest. Anyway the search by Bonnie's and George's parents ended in a motel in Bowling Green. George was befuddled for days after they returned. Bonnie got what she wanted and rejected any offer the Van Pelt family made to have the marriage annuled.

Helen broken hearted, left town and was never heard of again until this last reunion.

OK, I gave you a brief background. Now I'll tell you about the reunion.

The reunion was held on Bonnie and George's estate, a very beautiful place. It was a picnic affair in their yard with servants and all. There were over forty people, about half were classmates. We went through the usual routine of commenting on our beer bellies, bald-headed men and fat gray haired women, with big backsides, and anything else you can image. About an hour after the party began it happened!"

"What Happened?"

"A beautiful girl walked into the patio. She stood there for a moment. Bonnie's mouth fell open. She raised slowly with disbelief. She couldn't speak. I said, for heaven sake, it's Helen. After all these years and here she is. How wonderful to see her again. She walked toward us. I was stunned at her beauty. She looked so young. She had no weight problem, that was obvious. Her waist was that of a teenager. Her hair was still the shiny brown of her teenage days. It's hard to believe that a woman her age could still look so young. She was wearing a light blue chiffon dress with short sleeves and a white belt around her petite waist. The modest white collar gave her a look of a wholesome young girl. Her white high-heeled shoes stepped smoothly toward us. Now we could see her sparkling eyes. Her lips parted, bringing forth the warmest, friendliest smile I have ever seen. Every classmate came forward except Bonnie, she was still flabergasted.

For a while it was mass confusion. Everyone asking questions. Finally, we had Helen sitting down and answering questions. She left Detroit after graduation and went to Duluth to live with an aunt. It was there that she met and married a fine man by the name of Wade. He was a postal employee. He died of a heart attach four years ago and left her with a small pension. They had no children. George nervously rubbed his bald head and Bonnie continuously looked at George for support. They were in shock. To counter the praise being heaped on Helen, Bonnie walked close to her and stated, "Helen dear, do you realize that you have some gray hair?"

Helen laughed, "If you look closer you'll see a lot more gray hairs."

The others were moved with Helen's modesty. We were all preoccupied with how young she looked. This was soon verified when Bonnie's 20 year old son Paul walked up and said, "Mother who is the beautiful girl I saw walk into the yard?" It was Bonnie's turn to be thunderstruck. Her face became ashen white. Paul was the spitting image of his father of twenty some years ago. Helen kept starring at Paul. Bonnie could see what was taking place.

"She sees George in my son, I've got to get Paul away from Helen." She thought.

"Paul why don't you go out with your friend Tony, I'm sure you'd be bored with us old timers."

"Nothing doing Mom," Paul said, "Not as long as this doll is here. I'll call Tony and have him come over. Well Mom, are you going to introduce us?"

"Of course," Bonnie said, "Paul this is Mrs. Wade, Mrs. Wade this is my son Paul.

Mrs. Wade graduated from high school with your father and I.

"Mom's kidding of course," Paul said. "Who's daughter are you?"

"Your Mothers not joking Paul, I think you are." Bonnie felt a feeling of relief, but she shouldn't have.

"Mrs. Wade, can I get you something to drink?"

"Yes, Paul. Some punch will be fine." Bonnie left to circulate among her guests.

Paul returned and knelt down on one knee to hand Helen her drink. She purposely made their fingers to intertwine. They laughed about it, but then she stopped laughing and looked him straight in the eyes and softly said, "Thank you Paul." She could tell he was thrilled. Her timing was perfect.

Suddenly he was no longer the brash, casanova that he was with those young giddy girls that he was used to dating. He returned to the house utterly infatuated and Helen knew it.

The men gathered around Helen vying for her attention.

"Would you like another drink Helen? Are you comfortable Helen?"

Helen was careful to give each and everyone the same attention. This seemed to be very agreeable to the fellows as there was considerable laughter and comaraderie from the group. The ladies had quietly gathered across the lawn and were giving each other their opinion of what was taking place.

"I would never toy with men the way that she is," stated overweight Dorothy.

"I guess none of us would, that is, unless we could," said Mary. Bonnie stood up, "I'll bust up that private party right now."

"Helen dear, come with me. I want to show you the house and also give you a break from these schoolboys."

"What a beautiful home you have Bonnie. Thank you for the tour."

"You'r welcome Helen, I thought you would like it. I'm rather proud of our home.

Bonnie felt better, like she was now in control of things.

"Bonnie may I use your phone? I'd like to call my motel.

"Of course, use the phone in the den. I'll see you in the garden."

As Helen was thumbing through the telephone directory, she heard Paul and his friend Tony come in. They stopped in the hallway.

"Paul said, Tony I've got a problem getting to college in California. If I go by car

I'll have to leave tomorrow. I haven't been able to contact anyone heading that way. If I fly I'll have to leave some books behind, along with some other paraphernalia like my stereo equipment. Helen remained quiet until they left, making sure they wouldn't know that she had overheard their conversation.

Helen rejoined the party and waited for Paul and Tony to come into the garden.

She pretended not to notice them. Then in in a voice loud enough for Paul to hear she stated, "I won't be staying too late. I have a long drive ahead of me in the next few days.

"Where are you going Helen,? someone asked.

"To California to visit friends, They're expecting me.

"Holy cats," bellowed Paul. Helen turned to him with a look of bewilderment.

"Mrs. Wade, could I go with you? I've been trying for days to find someone driving to California. I'm going to U.C.L.A. and leaving tomorrow would be perfect.

"How wonderful," Helen said, I'll have someone to share the driving with. I was really dreading that long drive alone". Thing were going too fast for Bonnie. She wanted to shout no, but nothing came out of her mouth. Helen and Paul walked away from the group.

"Paul, I feel so secure knowing that you'll be with me." She placed her hand on his arm and looking him softly in the eyes and with all her alluring feminine charm, she said,"you'll be able to protect me then, won't you Paul?"

Like a trout taking the bait, he was hit and hit hard. With a

lump in his throat he stuck out his chin and said. "You bet I

will Mrs. Wade. I wouldn't let any harm come to you." Then

as an afterthough he said,

"I pump iron."

"Pump iron,?" Helen questioned.

"yes, I lift bar-bells. Been doing it for years."

"May I feel your muscle? Oh my, you are a man Paul.

From now on I want you to call me Helen."

Bonnie hadn't taken her eyes off them. She didn't like

what she saw. When Helen and Paul came back, Bonnie

ask, "what were you two talking about?" With a broad smile

on his face, Paul stated, "Helen and I are leaving for California tomorrow." Poor Bonnie, this wasn't her day.

"Helen- -Helen, You mean Mrs Wade I presume. Come in the house Paul, right now and I mean right now."

When Paul came out of the house he was sad. He walked directly to Helen, making sure no one could hear him. Weakly he explained that his Mother had other plans for his trip back to school. She wanted him to fly. He tried to utter other excuses, but Helen placed a finger on his lips.

"It's alright Paul," she said. "I'll ask your friend Tony to drive with me. He's laid off and could use some extra money."With a look of disgust, Helen said,"You do as your Mommy tells you." She turned and quickly walked away. She had thoroughly humiliated him. He was no longer her tall, handsome protector, just a litte boy. It was more than he could take. He ran after her pleading, "Helen, I'll go with you. We'll leave tomoorrow, I promise."

Helen paid no attention to him. She continued walking and sat in a chair where a large group conversing. Paul, was determined to re-establish his image with Helen and himself.

"Attention everyone", he shouted. "Tomorrow Helen and I are leaving for California." No one said a word. He felt foolish, but was also elated that he had the courage to say it.

Bonnies shoulders sagged. She was defeated, Helen had complete control over her son.

Helen sipped on her drink and with a smile on her face she looked directly at Bonnie and said."Paul dear, will you map our route so we can go through Bowling Green, Ohio? I have some business to attend to there." Bonnie dropped her drink.

"Bowling Green, oh no! She's planning on marrying Paul. Bonnie, in a daze, staggered over to Helen. "Helen may I see you in the house, Please, Please? Bonnie shut the door of the den and slid her heavy frame onto to the edge of the couch.

"Helen, please not my Paul. You have every right to want revenge for what I did to you, but to marry my son! Could you despise me that much.? He's so young Helen, only 20. Your'e old enough to be his mother. He's absolutely mesmerized by your sophistication and beauty. It kills me to see how helpless he is." Helen stood in the middle of the room motionless, her face without expression. Bonnie dropped to her knees, tears streaming from her eyes In a voice barely audible. She pleaded, "what do you want

Helen? Would you like George back? You can have him.. Do you want money? I'll give you a hundred thousand dollars, two hundred thousand, just let me have my baby back."

"Why should I Bonnie? Paul and I could have some happy years together. My age doesn't seem to bother him To me it's like turning the clock back, not many people can do that. By the way Bonnie, would you mind if I called you Mom?"

Bonnie looked at Helen with fire in her eyes. If looks could kill, Helen would be dead, then and there. There was silence, then Helen said, "How do I know your check won't bounce? How do I know I can trust you?" Bonnie looked up, a gleam of hope in her eyes. She teetered to her feet.

"Oh, Helen, I'll have a cashier's check for two hundred thousand dollars here in less than an hour," Helen walked to the door, and without looking back she said"ok, we'll see.

Forty-five minutes later Bonnie came back. There was Paul with his arm around Helen's waist. Bonnie froze for a moment," has Helen changed her mind?" The thought of Paul marrying her made Bonnie's heart beat faster. She caught Helen's eye and gave her a beckoning sign. Helen excused herself and approached her.

"Look in the envelope Helen." Bonnie was meek and overly polite, trying not to offend this majestic woman.

"You kept your word and now I'll keep mine. But, first I'm going to kiss paul good bye." Nervously, Bonnie said, "Could you kiss him on the cheek?" Helen's look was enough to make Bonnie quickly cancel this request.

"Of course, do whatever you want to do."

Helen explained to Paul that she wouldn't be going to Califoria. He seemed disappointed, but otherwise accepted her explanation. Everyone was watching them, wondering what was going on. As paul uttered his disappointment Helen turned her head so he couldn't see her moistening her lips."This will be a kiss he will never forget," she thought. As her face came close to his, her arms went around his neck. He picked her up lightly. They kissed. It was a lifetime for Bonnie. There were oohs and ahs from the group. Finally it was over. Paul let Helen down slowly and she immediately walked toward the flabbergasted guest.

"Would one of you gentelman please give me a ride to my motel? I must leave now, I would appreciate it so much."Danny volunteered, but his wife quickly canceled impulsive offer. Most men were very willing to drive her but their wives had a look in their eyes that said,"don't even think of it."

Mary was different, she spoke up, "Bert will drive you to your motel

Bert looked at Mary with surprise. He was one of the few who didn't care for the task.

Mary pushed him gently. "Go ahead Bert."

As they drove into the motel parking lot, Helen said, "Come to my room for a few minutes."

Bert was scared and it showed. Nervously he said,"Please Helen, I have to get right back.

"I said come in for a minute." It was more of a command than a request." I have a message for you to take back to Bonnie."

"But can't you tell me here?" he stammered. She looked at him sternly without saying a word.

"Ok," he said, "just for a minute," As Helen was unlocking the door bert was wringing his hands, "I think you should know

Helen, I'm under doctor's care."

"Shut up Bert. You always were a weak-kneed marshmallow. Now sit down over there and don't move."

Fifteen minutes later Bert was back in his car driving like a maniac. He managed to get back in one piece. When he came in the garden we could see he was vividly shaken.

"What in the world's the matter Bert,? you look terrible.

"Give me a drink," he said.

"But you don't drink," I said.

"Give me a drink, and I mean now."

Bert sat down and finished two whiskeys. As he calmed down, he said, "I have a message for you Bonnie, from Helen, and here it is. When we arrived at the motel I went to her room with her."

"Bert," Mary said with an air of shock."

"You rascal Bert," one of the guys shouted

"Now everyone shut up and let me finish. Helen more or less coerced me to go to her room. Anyway she told me to sit down while she stepped into the bathroom. I could see she was washing her face. This she did four or five times. Then the door closed.

A few moments later she came out and immediately threw something at me. It landed at my feet. It was a padded bra. She came closer. I couldn't believe what I saw! Her face was old and wrinkled. I wanted to scream."

"Are you shocked Bert?" Helen said with a big smile."Pancake make-up can do wonders for an old face."

Bert held up his hand and said, "wait there's more. She kicked off her shoes and began to laugh as she reached behind her waist and gave a tug. Her padded back-side fell to the floor. She gave it a swift kick, sending it through the air and bouncing it off the side of my head. She began laughing louder. Stepping over to the dresser she quickly removed her eye lashes, eye brows, and contact lenses. After putting on a pair of horn rimmed glasses she let her false teeth sink slowly to the bottom of a glass of water."

"Watch Bert," she said,

"Off came her wig, revealing short, gray, scraggly hair." She looked so old. Helen picked up a check and began waving it around as she danced and laughed."

"Tell Bonnie my day has come." she yelled as she she continued dancing and laughing.

"This was too much for me. I ran out of the room and down the hall. I could still hear her laughing when I reached the end of the corridor."

Mary jumped to her feet, and in a resounding voice shouted, "I propose a toast to dear Helen."

Everyone stood up, glasses raised high. Everyone, this, except Bonnie. She had fainted and laid on the grass like a beached whale, unnoticed for the moment.

Mary waved her glass,"May Helen know only happiness for the rest of her life."

The answer from the group immediate and loud.

"Hip-Hip-Hurray Hip-Hip-Hurray Hip-Hip-Hurray"

AN EVENING AT THE GRAVEYARD

By Maurice P. Roche

"Craig, you're not going jogging now are you?""Sure why not?"

"It's too late to jog in the cemetery, isn't it?""Well Ann they lock up the cemetery at five and it's only four now. I'll have time to run about three miles and be out of there in time, before they close. You know I have to run every day after school if I want to make the track team in spring. I really enjoy jogging in Mt. Olivet, especially in the winter.

"Why?"

"Because, it's getting dusk and there won't be any one in the cemetery but me. I like the feeling of being alone among the tombstones and the leafless trees with the snow on the ground. Do you think I'm wierd?"

"Yes, and by the way Craig, they mentioned on the radio a little while ago that there was a rabid dog loose in that area."

"Oh come on Ann, are you trying to scare me?"

"Honest, that's the true Craig, and I don't want my brother bitten by a dog, especially by a mad dog.

"Ok I promise not to jog with mad dogs. I've got to get going. See you a little after five."

"The first mile and a half will be at the Sullivan tombstone, and there it is up ahead. Jogging only three miles isn't much, but it's better than nothing.

Come to think of it today is winter solstice, the shortest day of the year. December 21st the first day of winter. Time to turn around at Sullivan's place. Gosh, the wind is really picking up. We could be in for a big storm. Oh well I'll be at the east gate soon and…. What's that! I'd better stop. Maybe my imagination is getting the better of me. That's a dog ahead and dogs are not usually in the cemetery. Sure Ann said a rabid dog was loose in the area, but the chance of this being the dog is small. I'm scared, I'll admit it. Be calm. I won't move until I'm sure. He's just walking aimlessly around. Holy cats! he's foaming at the mouth! That's enough for me. I'm getting out of here! I'll have to go all the way back to the west gate and I don't have much time before they lock the gates. Run faster! That dog is still coming this way and at a trot! I wonder if he smells my scent? I don't think I'll get to the gate on time, but if it's locked I'll climb over it; even if it is eight feet tall with sharp spike-like bar Ann was right. I should have stayed at home. It's too late for that kind of thinking. There's the gate up ahead. Yeah, it would be locked, oh well I'll climb over it. Boy that wind is getting stronger and colder. What's that? It looks like a big spark coming from the fence. There it is again! I've seen this happen before. A hot electrical wire is down on the fence somewhere and the whole fence and gates are electrified! I'm ready to panic! It's ok. Don't panic, don't panic, don't panic! ok, I've got to get to the guard office at the other side of the cemetery. I'll take a short cut instead of following the road. Be careful and watch. Don't twist an ankle, what a thought! Here I am sweating, running and wondering about that dog. Wait a minute, there he is ahead. I'll just stand here until he turns the other way. Good thing I'm down wind from him and the snow is blowing around. I'll ease my way over to the cross at that tombstone. There, just strectch my arms out and that darn dog won't know the difference. I don't know how long I can stand here with my arms strectched out pretending I'm crucified. I've got to start movin to keep warm. He's looking directly this way. When is he going to stop looking? I think he's wise, he's coming this way! He's still quite a distance off, but he can move faster than I can. I'll never make it to the gate house. Climb a tree? No, No, I'd freeze in no time. Oh I know, the mausoleum with the door open! I've jogged past that mausoleu hundreds of times. I used to say to my self, why is that door partly open? Maybe he got up and left and forgot to close the door. Where is that mausoleum from here? If I cut over to the left it should be pretty close. That dog is gaining on me and he acts like he means business! I'm sure that's the mausoleum up ahead. The door is on the other side. Please be open, it is. Watch it! slow down — slow down — Oh Oh my ankle — Oh no, I hope I didn't break it. No time to worry about that now. Hop around to the other side and see if the door is still ajar. It is! get in quick. There's no handle on the inside. Pull on the grating, pull, pull harder! It's stuck. Try again. The dogs coming! Pull, Pull. CLAN The door's shut and it"s locked! How do I open it? There's no handle, no latch, nothing! I've got a good view through the glass door but the grating on the door means I'm locked in. Scratch all you want dog. In fact you can huff and puff and I still won't let you in. HA HA

safe at last! "Fifteenth precinct, Office Ryan speaking. May

I help you?

"yes I'm worried about my brother. He went jogging in

Mt. Olivet cemetery and hasn't return.

"How long has he been gone lady?"

"About two and a half hours."

"What only two and a half hours! Lady if we started

looking for every person missing for a few hours, we

wouldn't have a police department left."

"You don't understand officer. My brother went to the

cemetery to jog. The cemetery closes at five. He must be

locked in. What really worries me is that rabid dog running

in that area. You know how dogs react to people running."

"Lady I think your overly concerned. Your brother

probably jogged over to a friends house and is sitting there

having a snack right now.'

"Let me talk to your superior!"

"Calm down lady. Give me your name and address and I'll have our car in that area keep an eye open for him. Now what's your name?"

"Ann O"Brien."

"And your address?"

"11090 Cottage."

"Ok Miss O"Brien Give me your telephone number."

"173 8941, Will you call me right back? I mean as soon as the scout car checks out the cemetery?"

"As soon as we find something out, we'll let you know."

"Thank you officer."

This mausoleum is like a refrigerator, Craig thought to him self. If I jog in place for five minutes every half hour, maybe that will keep me from freezing during the night. I wonder if I can do it.? I'd like to lay down on the floor and sleep, but those cement slabs are really cold.

Well I'll be! that dog is back again. He knows I'm here alright. Growl and bark all you want, this is not a dog house. I see he still has foam around his mouth. It's getting late and dark. What a crazy situation I'm cold, cold cold. I've got to do some thing. If I was in that casket my body heat would keep me warm. That's it, why not. Let's see if the lid will come up. Nope it's locked.

This feels like the lock. Now if I can find some thing to break the lock with. Oh! there's a name on the casket. It's awful hard to see; Dorothy Wilson. Well Dotty, if I can open the lid, we're going to have to cuddle up, otherwise I'll freeze to death. What can I use to break the lock with? Maybe I could pry up one of these cement slabs off the floor. This one against the wall seems to be a little loose. If I only had a knife. That's the trouble with us joggers; we don't carry any thing extra with us. It's coming loose. Boy oh boy it's heavy. Rest for a minute. That dog! I wish he'd stop growling and barking and get out of here! Well here goes, if this slab doesn't break that lock nothing will. Hold on Dotty it won't be long now. Bang—Bang—Bang! Hurray! there goes the lock. Nuts! the lid opens but, only about twelve inches because of the shelf above it. I'll have to move the casket out and towards me More hard work. The casket must be solid bronze. Move the top a little, move the bottom a litte; over and over. Watch when it gets near the edge. Careful. Try opening the lid now. Oh no it's sliding off the shelf! I can't hold it. IT's going to drop to the floor. O my arm, my arm! Oh help, my arm! It's broken: I know it's broken. Why didn't I just let it fall and get out of the way! What chance do I have now? My arm is broken and pinned between the casket and the shelf. The casket is standing almost straight up. It could possibly fall over on me. Holy cats! Dotty your one hundred percent skeleton! What's that noise? Something 's happening over where I removed the floor slab. What could it be? Listen, watch. I believe it's that dog digging underneath! Sure enough, he's digging his way in here! This is it! I've had it! Oh my God I'm heartly sorry for having offended thee. I wish I could remember how the rest of it went. OH for heaven sakes he's almost in. Those eyes are like flashlights. I can see the foam around his mouth, I am just petrified. He stands there puffing with the foam dropping from his face. Nice doggy! Nice doggy! How long is he going to stand there before he attacks? Give me your hand Dotty! sorry about this Dotty. Here doggy, have a bone. He's coming at me. Get away from my throat, Ahhhh, HELP! HELP! He's licking me, He's licking me! Ha Ha Ha He's licking me. That's whip cream around your mouth! your not a mad dog after all HA HA HA, whip cream! So the rabid dog turns out to be a friendly mutt with whip cream on his face. You scared the stuffings out of me doggy. Listen to me, I want you to go and fetch someone, understand? Fetch, Oh yes you do understand. Go fetch. Here before you go let me wipe your face or you'll be scaring some other poor soul. There go, go and fetch. By golly he does understand. That dog went back through the hole like he knew where he was going. It seems like a long time since that dog left. Maybe he doesn't know what I wanted him to do. I'm sure I couldn't last the night here. My arm is broken and pinned behind the casket. At least my arm is numb, even if I am freezing. What a way to go!

There's someone out there.

"Hello out there! I'm in here, HEL HELP "

"Hello Craig. Are you alright?"

"Not really. Just get me out of here!"

"We're going to pry the door open, watch out for glass that might come flying your way.

" Ok, but hurry! I'm freezing." "It didn't take you cops long to pop the door. You guys sure know what your doing. My arm is broken; becareful. By the way how did you know my name was Craig?"

"Your sister reported you missing. We would have been in the cemetery sooner but a high tension wire was down on the fence. Our scout car is nearby. We'll put you in the back seat with your dog."

"Yeah, I wouldn't want to leave this dog behind. He saved my life!

"Saved your life? How was that?

"I sent the dog to get help and he brought you guys back."

"No way. We were dispatched to check out a person being chased by a dog into a mausoleum. It seems that some guy was watching you from that apartment over there with his binoculars. He reported seeing a brown dog with white stripes on his front legs and foaming at the mouth chasing you."

Craig replied, "This dog is brown, he doesn't have any white on him at all. As for the foam, would you believe someone put whipped cream around his mouth! Where are you taking me?"

"We're taking you to General Hospital instead of Holy Cross because your sister is there, but first we'll stop at the east gate."

"Are you the foreman of the Edison crew?" the Officer ask.

" Yes, we're all done here now there's no danger, the wire is repaired and we're leaving. The Public Lighting Department has already left."

"What's the story on that dog laying there?" the Officer asked.

"The guy looking at him is a veternarian and he says the dog is rabid. The dog was electrocuted when he tried to go through the fence. "

"Hey lad, stay away from that dog" The Officer yelled.

"I only wanted to see if that was my dog Sir, but it's not. My dog doesn't have white stripes on his legs like this one does.

"When did you lose your dog?"

"I really didn't lose him. My brother heard that there was a mad dog near the cemetery so he took my dog and put whipped cream on his mouth and turned him loose."

"Well lad come over to my scout car and take a look at the dog in the back seat."

"Oh! Yes that's my dog, come here Dusty."

Craig said, "I'm glad you got your dog back, he's a terrific friend to have. I thought for a while that he might be mine."

"Excuse me nurse, now that I have a cast on my arm can I go home with my sister.?

"No Craig, the doctor wants you to spend the night here. It won't be too bad. I'll have a ham sandwich with a glass of milk and a piece of cherry pie sent up.

Would you like some whipped cream on your pie.?

ABOUT THE AUTHOR

Maurice Patrick Roche is of one hundred percent of Irish ancestry, born in Detroit Michigan on January 10th 1924. He attended St. John Berchman's grade school and Denby high school. He joined the Marines in World War II and fought on Guadalcanal and Tarawa. He was wounded three times. In 1946 He married Ellen Lane Boss, they have eleven children and twenty-four grand children. Maury was a pilot, and he did wing walking at air shows. He retired from the Detroit Fire Department as Chief of Communications after forty-three years service.